The Story of a Girl Band

The First Cut

By Nancy Krulik

GROSSET & DUNLAP • NEW YORK

For Danny, from whom I have no secrets.

Text copyright © 2001 by Nancy Krulik. Cover and insert photographs copyright © 2001 by David Croland. All rights reserved. Published by Grosset & Dunlap, a division of Penguin Putnam Books for Young Readers, New York. GROSSET & DUNLAP is a trademark of Penguin Putnam Inc. Published simultaneously in Canada. Printed in the USA.

ISBN 0-448-42580-7   A B C D E F G H I J

Chapter 1

"Okay, Janine Gutierrez, you're the first performer," Madame Charlotte announced in her faint French accent as she stood in the middle of the dance studio, her ever-present clipboard in hand. There was a collective sigh of relief from the girls who were not chosen to perform first. For them, there was always hope there wouldn't be enough time for their piece to be critiqued that day.

But for Janine, there was no such luck. She could feel the familiar sensation of nervous excitement building up in the pit of her stomach as she popped the CD into the player. Then she took her place in the middle of the floor and inhaled deeply. Finally, she nodded to Madame Charlotte. The teacher pushed the "play" button on the CD player, and the music began.

As the familiar sound of Madonna's "Ray of Light" filled the studio, Janine's body began to move—almost on its own. Janine had rehearsed this dance at least a hundred times in the past week. It was the first dance she'd ever choreographed. As the music whirred around her, Janine knew the song would always be special to her for just that reason.

The other girls in the studio watched with genuine awe as Janine performed her dance. As always, Janine seemed to be at one with the music. The rhythm of the song seemed to be literally moving her across the shiny wooden floor. Her movements were strong, yet fluid, almost effortless. That was the sign of a great dancer—one who worked so hard that it made it appear as if she wasn't working at all.

Janine was so involved with her dance that she was almost caught by surprise as the song came to an end. The sudden silence in the room seemed to shock her out of a trance. Janine caught her breath and stood erect in the middle of the room, her arms by her side. She tried not to look too nervous as she faced Madame Charlotte. This was the moment of truth. Madame Charlotte was not one to mince words—her criticism was sharp, and often without regard for the dancer's feelings. She rarely gave compliments; but when she did, you knew you'd truly done well.

Madame Charlotte slipped on the glasses that hung from a rhinestone-studded chain around her neck. She looked at her clipboard and studied her notes for what seemed like an eternity. Finally, she began to reel off her impressions. "You've obviously put a lot of work into your project," she told Janine. "You do need to smile a bit, though. Act like you're enjoying yourself. Still, I liked the way you integrated many of the things we've learned in class into your

2

routine. You've definitely improved the fluidity of your movements. Now we need to work on your lift. You need to raise your body even higher."

"It'd take a forklift to raise her butt."

The whispered sarcasm came from a group of dancers standing in the corner of the studio. The comment was just loud enough for Janine to hear—but managed to escape Madame Charlotte's ears.

Janine could feel her face growing hotter. The girl who'd made that joke had a distinct Chicago accent. Janine would know the voice anywhere. It was obvious that the comment had come from Daria Griffith. Janine blinked her eyes feverishly, determined not to let Daria see her cry this time. "Thank you, Madame," she murmured quietly. Then she turned and bolted out of the studio. The door slammed ominously behind her.

Daria's mischievous coffee-colored eyes shimmered with delight as she watched Janine exit. But her outward expression revealed nothing.

Madame Charlotte also stared at the door, but the dance teacher didn't say a word. It seemed strange to her that Janine would be so emotional after a generally positive review of her dance, but Madame Charlotte had worked with teenage girls long enough to know that their moods could never be predicted. "All right. Next up is Lexi Livingston."

As Lexi's music wafted out from behind the studio door, Janine sat slumped in the hallway, fighting back the tears. This should've been a happy moment for her. Madame Charlotte had given her high praise for her work. And yet, all Janine could focus on was Daria's biting comment about her weight.

It wasn't that Janine was heavy. When she'd lived at home in Florida, she'd looked pretty much like everyone else—even a bit better because her body was so muscular from dancing. Sure, she was top-heavy, but that ran in her family. Hers wasn't a traditional dancer's body, but Janine wasn't a traditional dancer. She was more from the Jennifer Lopez/Paula Abdul school. Janine liked jazz and hip-hop a lot more than ballet.

At home in Miami, Janine had felt so good about herself. Especially when she'd gotten that acceptance letter in the mail from the Professional Children's Boarding School. The school was the best of its kind in the country. Janine had been so excited about moving to New York and having the chance to work with the experts on her guitar-playing, singing, dancing, and acting skills. She'd had to audition four times to get accepted into PCBS—three times in Florida, and once during a long weekend in New York. But the effort had been worth it. Everyone in the country knew that kids who studied at PCBS went on to do great things in show business. Janine had never felt prouder of herself than the day she'd boarded the plane that would take her to New York's LaGuardia Airport, and to her new life.

But almost from the moment she'd touched down in New York, Janine's self-esteem had plummeted. It seemed to her that everyone who lived in New York City was pencil thin—especially the dancers at PCBS. In Janine's mind, the difference between her and the other girls was the most obvious when they were all dressed in identical skintight black leotards and pink tights. The others all seemed to have long, lean legs and slim hips. Janine was the only one with a more traditional female body. It was like that old Sesame Street song Janine had heard when she was a kid; "One of these things/Is not like the others . . ."

Daria's comment about Janine's figure had cut through her like a knife. The tears were flowing fast and furious now. Janine could feel them running down her cheeks, but she was helpless to stop them. In fact, she was so focused on Daria's criticism—and feeling sorry for herself—that she barely heard the studio door open.

"Janine, you can't let that jerk get to you all the time!"

Janine looked up to discover her friend Alyssa Wilkinson standing over her. She shrugged and tucked a wisp of her shoulder-length brown hair behind her ear. "I can't help it, 'Lyss. She's so mean. And besides, she's right! My butt is huge."

Alyssa sat down beside her friend. "No, she's not right," Alyssa disagreed. "You're gorgeous. And your butt is perfect for your body. You're just a better dancer than she is. That's what pisses her off. You know Daria hates it when anyone but her is in the spotlight."

"I guess," Janine allowed slowly.

"Not 'I guess,' 'I agree,'" Alyssa ordered.

"I agree . . . Ma'am," Janine said, letting out a little giggle as she gave Alyssa a mock salute. Alyssa smiled, knowing that she sounded just like her dad, Major Marcus Wilkinson of the U.S. Army.

"That's better," Alyssa assured her, seemingly completely unaware of the sarcasm in Janine's voice. Her hazel eyes focused on her friend's tearstained cheeks. "We'd better clean you up before you go back in there. The last thing we need is for Daria to know you were out here bawlin' your eyes out. Never let the enemy know they've gotten to you, Janine. You don't want them to think they have any power over you."

Janine sighed and followed Alyssa to the bathroom. That was definitely easier said than done.

"Hey, look at the bright side: at least you have something to write in that stupid self-expression journal Ms. Lawrence is making us keep for English class. I mean, what is with that woman? It is soooo hard for me to come up with some 'deep, meaningful truths', each and every week," Alyssa admitted to Janine.

"Not for me," Janine countered. "I like writing in my self-expression journal. It usually helps me get a handle on my emotions. And with Daria around, I need to do that pretty often."

Self-Expression Journal Entry

I can't believe I let Daria get to me again. I know that Alyssa's right: She's probably just jealous. But that doesn't make it any easier when she's mean like that. I wish I could be more like Alyssa—tough and made up of what she likes to call the Right Stuff. But I can't. That's just not me.

It's not like Alyssa doesn't know what it's like to be teased. Daria's been on her case a lot, too. I heard she was the one who stole Alyssa's sheet music right before the callback auditions for the solo part in the chorus. Good thing Mr. Miller was able to play the piece from memory.

Even though Alyssa knew it was Daria who stole the music, she never let on. She just made sure that Daria was the first to know she'd gotten the solo. Alyssa's not afraid of Daria. She's not afraid of anything. She's proud of who she is.

I wonder what it feels like to really and truly like yourself.

Janine

Chapter 2

"Will one of y'all test me on my vocabulary words?" Katie Marr asked the group of girls who'd gathered in the dormitory lounge late that same afternoon for a study group. The tall, blond Texan held out a sheet of lined paper, hoping someone would grab it from her. "There's nothing I hate more than memorizing stuff," she added with a slight moan.

Cassidy Sanders frowned in agreement. "I know what you mean. There's too much schoolwork at this place. At least when I was working on *The Kids Company* the tutors worked around my acting schedule. If I had too many lines to memorize they held back on the school stuff until things let up. Here I feel like I have to work my career around my schoolwork. We have this huge showcase to put on, and the general studies teachers are acting like we have all the time in the world for things like vocabulary and algebra. I think it's nuts. It's sure not the way it is anywhere else in the business, I can tell you that."

Daria rolled her eyes. "Gee, thanks for reminding

us, Cass. We'd almost had ten minutes to forget that you used to be on TV."

Cassidy blushed. She hadn't meant to brag. She was just making a statement. Other kids talked about what their lives were like before they'd come to PCBS. Why couldn't she? After all, she had starred in TV's top-rated Saturday morning kids' show for five years. Performing professionally was pretty much the only life she'd ever known. She'd made her first commercial, a thirty-second ad for a diaper rash cream, when she was just six months old. She'd been performing ever since. No one back home in California thought that was weird. There were millions of kid actors out there. Here on the east coast people weren't as obsessed with the business as they were back home. Still, Cass had figured the kids at PCBS would be on her wavelength. She was kind of shocked to discover she was the only kid with professional experience in her class.

Quickly Cass slipped an electric pink scrunchy off her wrist and gathered her short, dark hair into a ponytail. "Here, I'll test you, Katie," she volunteered, in an attempt to change the subject. "What does 'betrothed' mean?"

"Engaged," Katie replied.

"Figures she'd know that one," Serena Barkin said, giggling. She twirled a strand of her long red curly hair around her finger. "After all, she and Keith are practically engaged."

"We are not," Katie insisted. "We're just really in love, that's all."

"We guessed that," Serena teased. "I think it was that collage of photos on your wall that gave it away."

Katie shrugged. "Can I help it if I miss him? I mean, this is the first time we've been more than two miles away from each other since we were kids."

Cass sighed. "Better get used to it," she said knowingly. "If you want a career in the biz, you'll be traveling all the time—going on location, promoting albums, touring, and everything else. It's tough to keep up a relationship when you're a performer. Trust me, I know."

Katie didn't reply. But she knew there was a grain of truth to what Cass was saying. And she had a feeling Keith knew it, too. Katie wasn't even a professional singer yet, and already her career was putting a strain on their relationship. "Read me the next word," Katie said finally, trying to shake the negative thoughts from her head.

"'Gratitude,'" Cass read from the sheet.

"Thankfulness," Katie answered.

"Speaking of thankfulness, is anybody else going to be hanging around here over Thanksgiving?" Janine asked. "I'm not going to be able to get home for the holiday."

Melanie Sun stood up and stretched long. Her torn vintage Van Halen T-shirt rode up on her body and exposed her silver belly button ring. "Well, I'd invite you to my place, but you know . . ." Her voice trailed off pointedly as she focused her dark brown, almond-shaped eyes on a piece of dust on the edge of the couch.

None of the other girls questioned Melanie's reluctance. They all knew that Melanie's home was anything but Brady Bunch perfect. Melanie lived with her aunt and her three older cousins in a small, two-bedroom walk-up in Brooklyn. She'd moved in with them when she was in middle school, after her mom had gone into rehab for drugs and alcohol. Melanie's mom was clean now, but Melanie had opted to live at PCBS rather than move back in with her. And though her aunt had sincerely made it clear that Melanie could visit any time she wanted, she obviously preferred to have one less kid in her apartment.

Besides, Janine wasn't so sure she'd want to go to Melanie's for Thanksgiving, even if she were asked. Melanie had hung with a tough crowd while she was in Brooklyn. She was the first person Janine had ever met who had a tattoo—a red rose on her ankle—and who'd ever been to a rave. Melanie was the only one of her friends who'd found a way to move out of the old neighborhood. Janine wasn't sure she wanted to meet Melanie's old crowd. The truth was, though she found Melanie intriguing, Janine was a little afraid of her. All the girls were. Even Daria was nervous around Melanie. She was pretty much the only girl at the school Daria hadn't goofed on.

"How about you Hannah?" Serena asked in her soft Iowa accent. "I'm not going home until Christmas, and I would sure love a place to go to on turkey day." Serena wrapped her arm around Janine's shoulder. "I think you could find a place in that huge Park Avenue apartment of yours for two stranded classmates."

At first Hannah Linden didn't say anything. Her cheeks grew pink, and she stared awkwardly out the window. "I don't think I'll be able to bring anyone home with me right now. Mom probably wouldn't like that."

Serena was about to suggest that maybe Hannah could call her mom and just see if it might be okay, but something in Hannah's voice made her think that she just didn't want to talk about it anymore. "Hey, I didn't want to get you all upset," Serena told her. "I just thought that since you have a big apartment, you could have a couple guests for the holiday."

"Oh, you didn't upset me," Hannah assured her a little too quickly. "It's just that we have a whole lot of people coming already—my dad's business associates and stuff. My mother would kill me if I brought any friends home with me."

Serena had to choke back a laugh. Friends? Hannah didn't seem to really have any friends. It wasn't that she was mean or difficult the way Daria was; it was more that Hannah didn't seem to want to mix and mingle with the other girls at the school.

"Yuck! A whole night of listening to real estate moguls discussing mortgage rates. Now I know what I'll be grateful for on Thanksgiving—that I'm not at your place!" teased Susie Gregg, a petite blond-haired girl with large blue eyes. She turned and smiled at

Serena and Janine. "I'm pretty sure my mom'll let me bring you guys to my house in Pennsylvania. It won't be anything fancy, but we can watch the balloons and stuff on TV. And then afterward my mom'll serve a big turkey with all the trimmings, my three brothers will fight over who gets the drumsticks, and we'll probably forget the cranberries until after everyone's eaten. I can guarantee there'll be plenty to eat and you won't be bored by a whole lot of tired conversation about New York real estate."

Serena smiled gratefully at Susie. Her fun sense of humor always seemed to break the tension in any situation. But before Serena or Janine could thank Susie for her offer, Alyssa burst into the room carrying a huge stack of envelopes. "You guys are not going to believe this!" she cried out as she tossed the seventh floor's mail onto the table in the middle of the room. But before Alyssa could tell her story, the girls leaped from their seats and practically dove for the mail.

All the girls except Daria, that is. She knew from experience that there would be no letter waiting in that pile her. Her parents were high profile lawyers in Chicago. They worked almost constantly. There was no time in their schedules to dash off a letter to their only daughter. Not that they'd forgotten about her or anything. Often they'd have one of their favorite personal shoppers mail her a package from a local boutique or something, but since there were no boxes at mail call today, Daria knew there was nothing for her. She turned away from the other girls and focused her attention on pulling her tousled curls back from her face with a gold butterfly clip.

"Wait, you guys, don't open your mail yet," Alyssa warned as her friends grabbed at the envelopes that bore their names. "I just overheard something in Ms. Geoffries's office that will top any news you guys might've gotten from home! I'm telling you, this is big! I mean MEGA HUGE! You're never gonna believe it!"

Chapter 3

"Okay, spill it," Cass demanded as Alyssa stood practically bursting with excitement in the center of the room.

"You'll never guess in a million years," Alyssa teased as she closed the door to ensure a little privacy.

Cass reached into a huge bowl of popcorn and threw a handful of kernels at Alyssa. "You're right. We won't. So tell us."

Janine nodded. "Yeah, c'mon 'Lyss. You've got our attention."

Alyssa wiped the popcorn kernels from her gray knit sweater and smiled. "Okay, so here's the scoop. I was getting the mail in the main office when I heard Ms. Geoffries talking to one of the teachers inside her office. It's hard not to hear through those thin walls in there."

"We know," Daria exclaimed with an exasperated sigh. "Speed it up, Alyssa. This is not an Oscar acceptance speech. Just get to the point."

Alyssa grinned, obviously enjoying the tension

that was slowly building around her story. "Anyway, so Geoffries says"—Alyssa lowered her voice about three octaves so that she could sound just like the school's chain-smoking headmistress—"I don't want anything going wrong. This could mean a lot of wonderful publicity. We simply can't let the students know that Eileen Kerr is in the school. She wants the girls to remain as natural as possible. She needs to know that the personalities involved will be able to perform as a group."

Cass almost choked on her popcorn. "Did you say what I thought you said?" she demanded of Alyssa.

"Oh yeah," Alyssa assured her. "Eileen Kerr is coming to our school to look for girls for her latest group!"

Alyssa didn't need to fill the others in about who Eileen Kerr was. There wasn't a teenager in the world who wasn't aware of Omega Talent, Eileen's company. Omega had launched practically all of the groups on the Billboard Top 20! Eileen was legendary in the business for being able to spot talented teens and mold them into highly marketable—and profitable— pop groups. Eileen and her team of coaches did it all: They searched out the hottest songs, acted as vocal coaches, choreographed the dances, and booked their acts on the highest rated talk shows and international tours. Working with Eileen Kerr was a one-way ticket to the top. Several Omega groups had already shot past the Backstreet Boys and 'N Sync on the charts.

"What kind of group is she thinking of putting together?" Melanie asked anxiously.

"Geoffries didn't say," Alyssa replied. "I guess it's a pop group that sings and dances. That's pretty much what the whole Omega lineup is these days."

Hannah eyed Alyssa closely. "Are you sure you heard right?" she asked finally. "I mean, why would she be coming here to look for talent? Doesn't she usually work out of the west coast?"

Alyssa raised her hands beside her shoulders. "I don't know why she's decided to look for talent in New York," she remarked. "I only know what I heard."

"It does sorta make sense," Serena suggested. "I mean, maybe she wanted to look at girls from all over the country. We're all from different places and we're all pretty talented."

Susie giggled. "Sort of like one-stop shopping, you mean."

"Leave it to you to bring shopping into it," Janine teased. "You shop-a-holic."

"But you guys can't tell anyone else in the school about this," Alyssa reminded them. "This info is just for girls who live on our floor. Strictly confidential, 'kay?"

"Well, that means you have to let me tell Lexi," Serena insisted. "She's my roommate, after all."

"Where is Lexi, anyway?" Alyssa asked.

"I think she went to the movies with that guy she met in the Village last week," Serena said. "You know, the guy with the Porsche?"

Melanie snickered. "Figures."

"What does that mean?" Hannah asked. "What's wrong with owning a Porsche?"

"Nothing," Melanie replied, idly running her hand over the rose tattoo on her ankle, "if you're the one who owns it. It's just that Lexi will only date guys who have Porsches."

"Or Mercedes, or BMWs, or Ferraris," Alyssa added.

The girls were so busy discussing Eileen Kerr's arrival and Lexi's love life that no one seemed to sense that Cass had quietly slipped out of the room for a while. But they all noticed her when she returned. Suddenly the long, lean brunette looked tired and stressed out. Her face had a gray tint to it, and her usually sparkling brown eyes seemed distant and unfocused.

"You okay, Cass?" Janine asked her.

Cass adjusted her size zero capri jeans. "Me? Oh, yeah. Sure. I just . . . um . . . had to go to the bathroom. All that buttered popcorn must've gotten to my stomach."

"There's no butter on the popcorn," Janine countered. "I made it plain this time."

"Oh well, I guess I'm just feeling a little under the weather, then. Some stomach bug or something." She forced a smile to her lips. "I'd better perk up if I'm going to make a good impression on Eileen Kerr, huh?"

The others nodded. They were all going to have to be at their very best for the next couple of weeks.

Susie turned to Katie. "You've been awfully quiet

through all of this, Cowgirl," she remarked, using her pet nickname for her friend. "Aren't you excited about the prospect of being in one of Eileen Kerr's groups?"

"Yeah, sure," Katie replied in a decidedly unenthusiastic voice. "I mean, who wouldn't be?"

But the truth was, Katie had barely given any thought to the idea of Eileen Kerr visiting PCBS. She was too focused on the opened letter sitting in her lap. It was from Keith. By now, his thick, back-slanted, lefthanded script was as familiar to Katie as her own handwriting. Keith never e-mailed Katie. He either called or sent her long, hand-written notes. He said it was more personal that way. So Katie sent Keith her letters by snail mail as well. She didn't want him to think she loved him any less than he loved her. She wanted him to know that he was always on her mind.

Although she'd only read the letter once, Keith's words were already seared into her consciousness like a cattle brand. She felt the ever-growing lump in her throat begin to turn to tears as the words rang through her brain. She blinked furiously to stop the burning sensation that was building up in her eyes.

"It's time to come home, Katie. You're not the show business type. You're too sweet and naive to be a part of all that. New York City is a tough town. It's bound to eat a sweet yellow Texas rose like you alive. Sooner or later, the constant rejection is going to tear you apart. It's killing me knowing that you're up there alone, setting yourself up for a fall."

19

Katie had to admit that, once again, Keith knew her as well as she knew herself. Lately she had been feeling a little homesick. All she'd really wanted was to jump on a horse and ride for miles under the hot Texas sun. And she'd been worrying a lot lately about what she was going to do after she graduated from PCBS in the spring. She'd be all on her own in New York City, probably going from audition to audition like every other ambitious performer who'd set foot on the island of Manhattan. What if Keith was right? What if she wasn't one of the lucky ones Eileen Kerr picked to be part of her new group? Could she deal with the rejection? And would that rejection be the first of many to come?

Katie's self-doubting thoughts were interrupted by a knock at the door. One of the dorm supervisors was standing outside the study lounge.

"Hannah, there's a phone call for you on the hall phone. I think it's your mom,"the supervisor told her.

"Oh my! Is Mumsie calling from Paris again? Or is it Rome this time? I simply can't keep up with her schedule." Melanie put on a fake, snobby British accent to mock Hannah.

Hannah blushed, and for a moment she looked as though she was about to cry. But she didn't respond to Melanie's baiting. She simply left the room to take her phone call.

"That girl really gets to me," Mel moaned. "I mean, she's always off by herself. She never hangs out with any of us. It's like she thinks we're not worthy of her or something."

None of the other girls could argue that point with her. Hannah was a little standoffish and cold. But most of the others just assumed that that was the way girls from New York society were raised. Still, no one could deny that Hannah was talented. Even with all her money, she'd earned her place at PCBS fair and square. Nobody'd bought her a space at the school. She worked as hard as anyone else. And that was something the rest of the girls could respect about Hannah, even if they didn't really like her personally.

"Well gang, I hate to break up this little party, but I promised to meet a friend of mine in the East Village for a burger," Melanie announced suddenly as she scooped up her books and headed toward the hall. "If I'm going to be in shape for Eileen Kerr, I'm going to need some serious food. Not that slop they serve in the cafeteria."

Serena stopped her friend at the door. "Hey Mel, don't forget to be in by curfew," she whispered quietly in her ear. "The last thing any of us needs is a demerit on her record now."

Melanie nodded and laughed. When it came to following the rules, Serena was the perfect angel. "I'll be home before the subway turns into a pumpkin, fairy godmother. I promise."

Serena smiled. "Oh, I'm not your fairy godmother," she insisted. "But I sure hope Eileen Kerr turns out to be mine."

Self-Expression Journal Entry

Note to Ms. Lawrence: I'm trying to be as honest as I can in this journal. If you read this, I'm counting on you to keep your promise and make sure this all stays confidential.

Lately I'm beginning to resent it when my mother calls me at school. That's a life I've left behind. I've created a whole new me; someone sophisticated and totally in-the-know. I don't like it when I hear my mother's voice. It's not that I don't love her or anything; it's just that when she calls, I sorta have to face the truth about who I really am.

Not that I love everything about this new, more sophisticated, me. I mean, I really wish I could've taken Janine and Serena home with me for Thanksgiving. But what would I have said—"you guys can go hang out in my tiny closet of a room in the servants' quarters while I help my mom serve a bunch of rich jerks their Thanksgiving dinner"?

I can't let these kids know that my mom is just a maid, and that we only live on Park Avenue because that's where her boss, David Alden, lives. Never mind the fact that not only hasn't my dad built a real estate fortune, I've never even met my dad. He ran out on my mom when she got pregnant with me. If they knew the truth they'd all feel sorry for me. And I couldn't deal with their pity. I see how they all look at Melanie when she talks about her mom and her old neighborhood. I couldn't bear it if they looked at me with the same condescending compassion. I'd rather have them hate me than feel sorry for me.

Anyway, my Thanksgiving is going to be the worst. My mom is able to suck in her gut and take the crap the Aldens dish out, but I can't. I don't know how she does it—it tears me apart to see them order her around. That's gonna make it a long four days. But hey, at least I know I'll be coming back here, to my new life. That's more than Mom can say.

Besides, Thanksgiving is a few weeks away. I don't want to think about it until I have to. There are much more exciting things to focus on around here.

I've just got to be picked for Eileen Kerr's new band. That way I can make some real money, and finally get my mom out from under the Aldens' control. It's the only way I'm going to become what everyone else around here already thinks I am.

Hannah

Chapter 4

It took Melanie only a minute before she spotted her best friend, Julia, in the crowded coffee shop on Waverly Place. She was sitting at a small table way in the back, but she was hard to miss—her long, stick-straight hair was dyed a bright cantaloupe color.

"Nice hair," Melanie complimented her as she slid into the chair across the table from her pal. "When'd you do it?"

"Last week," Julia replied, running her fingers through her orangey-pink 'do. "I was getting tired of the blue. I wore it this way to the rave in the old tire factory on Eighteenth Ave. It was a megahit. You, of course, weren't there to see it!"

"Sorry," Melanie apologized as she picked up a menu. "I had a vocal exam the next morning—if I was up dancing all night, my voice woulda been total shit the next day."

Julia rolled her eyes. "Boy, have you changed. You never used to care so much about grades before. Especially if there was a party to go to! And let me tell you, this was a major PARTY!"

Melanie nodded. "Sorry I missed it. But I guess I have changed a little. It's just that I've never been in a school like this before. I mean, imagine having a test in singing!"

Julia didn't answer. Melanie's love of all things PCBS was getting pretty tired as far as she was concerned. It'd been almost two years since Melanie had scored that scholarship to PCBS and moved on up to Manhattan. Julia was growing bored with hearing how much Melanie loved her fancy boarding school in TriBeCa while she was still stuck in the same old Brooklyn public she'd been going to since freshman year—the one the press called "Hell High." The reporters weren't so far off: The school was filled with too many kids, too many gangs, not enough books, and a bunch of frustrated teachers who were too afraid of the kids to actually teach them. It was like the poster school for urban decay. All their lives the girls had been inseparable. But now only Mel had gotten a one-way ticket out of Hell High.

For a long while, both seventeen-year-olds stared at their menus as though they were the most fascinating things in the world—which was pretty absurd, considering they practically knew them by heart. The silence between them grew larger and stronger—something that never used to happen when they were kids. Before Melanie had moved to PCBS, there was always something to say, someone to gossip about, some news to spread. But now . . .

Finally, it was Melanie who felt the need to break the wall of silence. "You're not going to believe what's happening at school now!" she exclaimed in an overly excited loud voice. "It's amazing!"

"Let me guess," Julia asked in a sarcastically bright sitcom kind of voice. "They've named you homecoming queen, and you get to ride on a float at the big game!"

Melanie scowled. "Nice one, Julia. No, really. This is huge. You'll never guess who's coming to talent scout for her next group at PCBS! Eileen Kerr. Can you believe it?"

But Julia didn't seem particularly excited at her best friend's news. "What's that got to do with you?"

Melanie seemed confused. "What do you mean? It's got everything to do with me. I mean, she's going to pick some of us to be in her next group. Stardom, here I come!"

Julia shook her head and let out a haughty laugh. "Like I said, what does that have to do with you? Have you seen any of those Omega bands Eileen Kerr has put together? They're like a bunch of Barbie dolls singing about precious puppy love crushes. A gaggle of Susie Sunshines. Have you looked in the mirror lately? When's the last time a girl in an Omega group had a hole in her nose and a tattoo on her ankle? And since when did any of Eileen Kerr's people come from a neighborhood like ours? Take my advice, girlfriend. Forget about Eileen Kerr. She'll probably take one look at you and run like hell!"

Melanie frowned and kicked at the brown spotted floor by her feet. She'd been so caught up in the enthusiasm of the upbeat girls at school that she hadn't been able to see things clearly. That kind of thing happened to her a lot lately. She was spending so much time around all of those bright-eyed, daydreaming "Hey, let's put on a show, gang!" types at PCBS that she was beginning to think she was one of them. But she wasn't. They were all the daughters of supportive parents who'd paid a lot of money to feed their daughters' dreams. Some of them might be richer than others, but they were all pretty much alike.

Melanie was different from them. And it took someone like Julia to remind her that she was really just a street girl who was at the school on scholarship. "A high-class charity case" was actually how Julia liked to put it. In Melanie's mind, Julia was kind of like medicine. What she said might taste awful going down, but in the end it made you right again.

Julia could see the disappointment in her friend's expression. She softened her voice and looked into Melanie's sad, dark eyes. "Look, M, you're the most talented person I know. And you're probably gonna be the only one of us who'll break out of the neighborhood. But this isn't the way, y'know. You've got a harder edge, and there's a market for your sound. You'll get your shot. Just not this time." Julia folded her menu and slipped it back behind the ketchup container. "Hey, I'm not that hungry, anyway. You wanna go dancing or something? There's a new club on Avenue A that's supposed to be really smokin'."

Melanie nodded quietly. Maybe dancing was just what she needed. Who cared if she missed curfew? She had a lot more than a demerit going against her when it came to making a good impression on Eileen Kerr and her Omega flunkies.

It was almost two o'clock in the morning when Melanie snuck up the fire escape and forced the partially opened seventh-floor lounge window up just enough for her to crawl through. It was a trick Melanie had discovered when she'd first arrived at PCBS, and she'd been using it to break in after curfew ever since. Her only fear was that one day the dorm chaperones were going to catch on and lock the window.

But the "wardens" hadn't managed to figure out Melanie's secret passageway yet, and as she tiptoed her way down the dimly lit hall to her room, she felt quite superior to the other girls who she knew had been fast asleep in their dorm beds for quite a while. She may not have been Eileen Kerr material, but when it came to street smarts, Melanie was at the top of her class. No one ever seemed to catch on to the fact that she wandered in and out of the school whenever she pleased.

Until tonight.

Suddenly a tall figure leaped out from behind a dorm room door and grabbed Melanie tightly by the arm. Mel gasped in terror. Who the hell was this?

"Well, it's about time!" a girl with a heavy Atlanta accent hissed angrily. "I've been waiting all night."

Melanie breathed a silent sigh of relief. She could feel the muscles in her arm loosen in her captor's grip as she came to the realization that it was only Lexi who'd managed to catch her sneaking in after curfew.

"You nearly scared me to death!" Melanie scolded her through a carefully muffled whisper. "What're you doing up?"

"Waiting for you, you party animal," Lexi replied. "Where'd you go?"

"I'll tell you about it in the morning," Melanie vowed. She covered her mouth with her hand to muffle a yawn. "Right now, I've gotta get a couple hours of sleep. I've got that Shakespeare seminar first period. If I'm not rested, I'm liable to fall into a midsummer's night dream right at my desk."

"Real cute," Lexi scowled. "I'll let you go off to dreamland in a second. But right now I need you to do me a favor."

"What?"

Lexi shook her head. "We can't talk about it here. Little Miss Rule Book is liable to hear." She pointed inside the room where Serena was tucked away under her covers. "Let's go into the lounge."

Melanie followed Lexi to the study lounge and flopped down on the couch. "All right, whaddaya want?" Melanie demanded as she whipped off one of her shoes and rubbed her tired toes.

"I want y'all to help me sneak out tomorrow night after curfew," Lexi demanded, her usually sweet,

Scarlett O'Hara-like accent suddenly sounding more like a command from General Lee.

"What do you need me for? Just go out before curfew. If you're late getting back, ring the bell. Someone'll let you in."

"Oh sure," Lexi countered. "And give me a big fat demerit for it. That's all I need, a whole weekend stuck in this place. No, I want help from an expert, someone who knows this city well, to help me out."

"What's so important?"

Lexi sat beside Melanie on the couch—so close that her tousled blond hair brushed Melanie's cheek. "I found out where Eileen Kerr and the coaches are staying this week," she confided.

Suddenly Melanie was interested, in spite of herself. "How'd you do that?"

Lexi drew her cream-colored satin robe close around her. "I called my cousin the computer nerd back in Marietta. He tapped into Geoffries's Palm Pilot and got Eileen Kerr's local number."

"Are you nuts?" Melanie exclaimed. "You had someone hack into the headmistress's personal files?"

Lexi shrugged. "Hey, if she wanted them protected, she should've secured 'em. Anyway, don't you want to know where they're staying?"

Melanie hesitated.

"At the Plaza, of course," Lexi told her, not giving her time to respond. "Where else? Anyway, Eileen, her scouts, and Ms. Geoffries are having dinner at the hotel tomorrow night at nine. I figure they should be out of dinner by ten-thirty. Then Ms. Geoffries will leave, and I'll get a chance to 'accidentally' bump into Eileen in the lobby." Lexi caught Melanie's dubious glance. "Er, I mean we'll get the chance," she corrected herself.

"But then you could never get back here by curfew," a small voice interrupted the two girls.

Melanie looked up to discover Serena at the door. She and Lexi had been so into their conversation, they'd never heard her walk in the room.

"Oh God," Lexi muttered under her breath.

"Serena's right," Melanie agreed, happy to have an excuse for backing out of Lexi's scheme. "I don't want to be late for curfew."

Serena looked at Melanie's coat and hat. "At least not two days in a row, right?"

Melanie furrowed her brow. "And your point is?"

Serena looked sadly into Melanie's eyes. "You promised you'd be back on time. You're just lucky you didn't get caught sneaking in."

Lexi turned to Serena and smiled with all the sincerity of a carefully trained southern belle. "Serena, sweetie, can't we just keep all this between us? I mean, it doesn't really affect you."

Serena didn't answer right away. Lexi couldn't be sure what her ever-so-honest roommate was thinking, so she knew she had to act fast. "Why don't you come along?" Lexi asked Serena, as genuinely as possible.

"What?" Melanie demanded with surprise.

"It makes perfect sense," Lexi explained. "Serena will make sure we leave in plenty of time to get back by our Friday night curfew. That's twelve o'clock instead of ten-thirty, right? And she'll get a chance to meet Eileen Kerr ahead of time, too. So we all benefit."

Serena thought about that for a moment. It wasn't often that Lexi invited her in on one of her adventures. In fact, this was the first time it had ever happened. Which, of course, made the whole thing suspect. And yet, Serena couldn't help but be excited. "All right," she agreed enthusiastically. "It's a date. Now get to bed, you guys. It's almost three o'clock!"

As Melanie and Lexi followed Serena down the hall, Melanie whispered in Lexi's ear, "I hope you know what you're doing."

Lexi nodded. "Believe me, I do."

English 201: Journal Entry

You're not going to believe what I had to do tonight. I actually had to ask Little Prissy Perfect to come with me when I go out tomorrow night. It was my only choice. I figure if Serena's in on the plan, she won't be able to squeal to Geoffries about my being out after curfew. Of course, I let her think we'd all be back right on time, but that's never gonna happen. In fact, if things work out the way I want them to, I won't be back until the next morning. I'll probably get a demerit or something, but by then it won't matter. If everything goes as planned (and you know I'll make sure it will), by the time the weekend is over I'll be on my way toward becoming Eileen Kerr's next shining star.

Ciao for now,

Lexi

Chapter 5

Melanie dragged herself down to breakfast the next morning, along with most of her friends. She was exhausted, and sleeping through the morning munch-out had seemed like a good idea when her alarm clock buzzed. But after many taps at the snooze button, her head began to clear and she realized that she had to make an appearance in the cafeteria. She didn't want to bring any attention to herself after her late arrival the night before, especially since there was a good chance she'd be missing curfew again tonight—along with Serena, of all people. What the hell had Lexi been thinking, asking her to come out with them? Serena was a good kid, but she was so damn honest! "Risk-taker" wouldn't exactly be the first word Melanie would've used to describe her. Somehow Melanie couldn't see Serena climbing up a fire escape and sneaking through a window in the middle of the night.

This was not going to be good. There was gonna be trouble. Melanie could feel it in her bones.

But for now, Melanie tried to focus on her first-period Shakespeare class. She'd planned on reading the second act of *As You Like It* last night when she got back from dinner with Julia. But her plans had obviously changed. Now she had only a few minutes in a noisy cafeteria to catch up. Quickly, she flipped open her textbook and tried to focus. But before she could read a word, Susie and Alyssa flopped down beside her. Susie seemed a little quiet, just like she did every morning. Alyssa, on the other hand, was in her workout clothes, and as cheery as could be. "Good morning!" she shouted brightly as she poured a container of milk into her Lucky Charms.

"What're you so happy about?" Melanie asked her.

"I don't know," Alyssa shrugged. "I'm just in a good mood. I had a great workout in the studio this morning."

Susie looked at her red and blue Swatch. "It's only seven-thirty," she muttered. "When did you have time to work out?"

"Oh, I've been up since five," Alyssa told her. "I always get up then. It's like I've got an internal wake-up call or something."

Susie laughed. "You can take the girl away from the army, but you can't take the army out of the girl."

Alyssa crunched on a spoonful of blue and yellow marshmallows and nodded. "Something like that," she agreed.

Just then Hannah slid into the seat beside Alyssa. "Have any of you seen Cass?" she asked, trying to be friendly, even though her voice was as cool and measured as always. "We were supposed to go over some notes this morning before our Business of Music class."

"I think she said she was skipping breakfast this morning. She wanted to sleep in or something," Susie replied.

"Cass skipping a meal? That's new and different," Melanie replied sarcastically. Then she began to sing to a fast, punk-esque tune: "It's time to go down for a meal, to eat a little dinner. But I just stay here in my room, getting thinner, thinner, thinner!"

The girls all laughed at Melanie's obvious commentary on Cassidy's eating habits. But their laughter was hollow. Each of them had their suspicions about Cass's sudden bouts of nausea or need for a few extra hours of sleep. They were all just too afraid to voice them.

Suddenly, Ms. Geoffries's distinctively throaty voice rang out over the intercom system. "Ladies, first period has been canceled," she announced. "Instead, we will have an all-school meeting in the Ethel Merman Theater in fifteen minutes. Anyone not present will receive one demerit."

Alyssa took a last bite of her cereal and grabbed her tray. "I'll go wake Sleeping Beauty on my way to the assembly," she told the others. "No one needs a demerit right now."

As Alyssa walked off, Janine looked at the others. "Ms. Geoffries certainly made this one sound important," she noted. "What do you think this whole assembly thing's about?"

"Probably the Fall Showcase. There's a lot to get done before the show," Susie suggested.

"There's only one way to find out," Melanie countered as she slipped her Shakespeare text into her backpack and breathed a sigh of relief. Class had been canceled. Now she had a whole weekend to catch up on her reading for class. "Let's get going."

Janine and Susie each took one last bite of breakfast and then trailed Melanie out of the cafeteria and downstairs to the theater.

It took a while to get the entire PCBS student body settled into the school's state-of-the-art theater. But once all of the 150 girls seemed to be in their places, Ms. Geoffries stood onstage and began to speak.

"It has come to my attention that someone has been spreading rumors about music mogul Eileen Kerr coming to visit our school," the headmistress said in a slow, determined voice.

A murmur bristled through the crowd. It was obvious that many of the students hadn't heard the same rumors the girls on the seventh floor had.

"Nobody is quite sure where this tale began," Ms. Geoffries continued.

Janine glanced over toward the left section of seats, where Alyssa, Cass, and Daria had all planted themselves. Alyssa was staring at the floor, trying desperately not to laugh. She certainly knew where the Eileen Kerr rumor had gotten started.

"But unlike most rumors, this one indeed has its

basis in truth," the headmistress revealed finally. "Ms. Kerr is coming to our school. It was my hope that her visit could be kept a secret—especially because I want all of you to remain focused on the Fall Showcase— but that was not to be. My goal today is to dispel any untruths that may be floating through the school. Ms. Kerr and a few of her Omega talent music and dance coaches will be visiting the school for the next few weeks. Currently, Ms. Kerr is searching for girls to be part of a new band she is planning to create called No Secrets. She thinks she will find the girls for her band here. The plan is for eight girls to be chosen initially. Those eight girls will go off to live in a brownstone owned by Ms. Kerr's Omega Talent company, and work on their singing and dancing techniques—while continuing their general studies. Eventually four of those eight girls will become members of Ms. Kerr's new pop group. With parental permission, of course."

"Of course," Alyssa muttered under her breath, wondering if her oh-so-tightly-wound military father would ever give her permission to do something as wild and exciting as travel the world with a pop group.

"No Secrets, huh?" Cass giggled into Alyssa's ear. "Perfect for you—you're the one who blew this secret out of the water in the first place."

Alyssa had to laugh in spite of herself. "Great name, isn't it?" she commented.

Cass nodded. "Did you expect anything less, coming from Eileen Kerr?"

Ms. Geoffries waited for the excitement in the

room to die down. "Girls, I don't want you to forget that we still have a showcase coming up. That is where your focus has to remain. If you need an added incentive to continue working on your individual showcase performances, let me inform you that Ms. Kerr and her team will be attending the show before they announce the eight finalists."

Daria smiled to herself. So Eileen Kerr really was coming to PCBS. For once, it had paid to be on the same floor with Alyssa. Daria had gotten a head start on thinking about how she was going to impress the Omega Talent team. She already had an entire plan in her head. All she had to do now was put it into motion.

That afternoon, Daria waited for Janine outside of the dance studio door. "Can I talk to you for a minute?" she asked as sweetly as possible.

Janine looked skeptical.

Daria nodded. "I don't blame you for not trusting me. I've been pretty mean to you lately."

Janine laughed. "Lately? How about since I got here?"

"You're right. I haven't been particularly nice to you. But I get that way when I'm jealous," Daria confessed.

Janine stared at her incredulously. "Jealous?"

"Of the way you dance," Daria continued. "And of the way everyone loves you. Nobody likes me."

"Maybe they would if you were a little less obnoxious," Janine suggested, apparently unmoved by Daria's confession.

"Maybe," Daria agreed. "Look, I have this idea for the showcase, and I was wondering if, well, if you weren't working with a team yet . . ."

"You want to work with me?" Janine asked.

Daria nodded. "I was thinking of asking Susie, too. It's this great idea for a dance number. I thought we could do a medley of a few disco songs from the seventies. Eileen Kerr's bands tend to do a lot of remakes of seventies tunes—like that group that did "Build Me Up Buttercup." This way we could show her that we are up to the kind of challenge Omega Talent expects. Whaddaya think?"

Janine paused. It was a good idea. That was no surprise; Daria often had good ideas. The problem was her ideas always benefited Daria. Which meant that she had to have an angle here, as well.

But for the moment, Janine couldn't think of how anything Daria was saying could hurt her. Besides, being on Daria's team would mean that for a few weeks at least Daria would lay off her. And Susie would be there as well to act as a buffer zone if Daria got too wild or cruel.

"Why don't you talk to Susie, Daria?" Janine answered finally. "If she says yes, then I will, too."

Self-Expression Journal Entry/November

I know this is my first journal entry for the month, but I was waiting until I had something really worthwhile to put in here. And now I do. Sometimes I amaze myself with just how smart I really am. In the past, some of my plans have been nothing short of prize-winning material. But today, I topped even me. I managed to convince Janine and Susie to do a song-and-dance routine with me for the showcase.

Now before you think I've gone absolutely insane—asking the class chub and a girl who's singing pipes are a little rusty to back me up—think about the benefits of having those two in my number. It actually makes a ton of sense. I mean, next to Janine, I'll look absolutely model thin on stage. And the girl really can dance (maybe even better than I do—some of the time), so she'll be very helpful when it comes to having the best choreography in the showcase.

As for Susie, well sure, she's pretty—if you like that wide smile and freckly natural look. But since her singing isn't the greatest, my voice will sound even better than it usually does when Eileen Kerr hears it next to Susie's.

Look, it's not like I'm being mean to the two of them or anything. Neither one of those losers actually has a shot at being picked as one of the eight finalists, anyway. At least with my plan they get a chance to be onstage with someone who has real star potential . . . me!

Maybe after I make the top eight, Mom and Daddy will finally take what I'm doing seriously. Maybe they'll even have to pay attention to my career for a change. After all, with Eileen Kerr backing me up, the rest of the world sure will be paying attention to me.

Gotta run,

DARIA

Chapter 6

Melanie stood quietly in the school lobby waiting for Serena and Lexi to come down and meet her. The girls were late. Melanie adjusted her funky, black polyester shirt and ran her hands over the front of her velvet skirt. As usual, Melanie had managed to take thrift shop bargains and turn them into a look that was all her: chic and sophisticated, with a little exotic fun thrown in for good measure.

"Okay, are y'all ready?" Lexi asked as she came gliding out of the elevator with Serena in tow.

"Are we ready?" Melanie moaned. "I've been waiting for you guys for ten minutes already." She looked at Lexi and Serena and began to laugh.

"What's so funny?" Lexi demanded. "I'll have you know that I got this outfit at Rue de Reves. That's the hottest boutique in SoHo."

"I'm sure," Melanie replied. "It's just that . . . well . . . look at us!"

Lexi and Serena had to laugh. There was Mel in her thrift store chic. Serena was dressed in Banana

Republic casual: a gray blouse tucked into a straight, khaki-colored skirt. And Lexi had outdone herself, wearing a little black skirt and a tank top under a loosely knit, form-fitting sweater. The see-through sleeves made her arms look sexy and added a little bit of Goth danger to the ensemble. She'd finished off her look by pulling her shoulder-length blond hair back with a thin headband.

"What's that perfume you're wearing?" Serena asked Lexi.

Lexi lifted her arm and held a tiny charm bracelet up to Serena's nose. "It's not perfume. It's scented pellets that are hidden in this charm, see? That way, the scent doesn't wear off early in the evening. This one's call Seduce Me."

Melanie raised her left eyebrow suspiciously. That didn't exactly sound like something you would wear for a first meeting with the woman who could someday make you a star. It was obvious to her that Lexi had something else in mind. The question was, what? "Well, let's get going," Melanie suggested. "We don't want to miss Eileen Kerr."

"Or bump into Ms. Geoffries," Serena reminded her.

"Right," Melanie agreed. "Let's take the B train. It'll let us off near the Plaza."

Lexi shook her head. "You want to take the subway?!" she scoffed. "Not me. Let's get a cab."

Melanie blushed. These were the moments she hated—the ones where she suddenly felt different from the other girls in the school. There was no way she could afford to take a cab up to Central Park South.

"It's on me," Lexi said cheerily as she reached out her hand. "I just got my allowance."

Melanie didn't say a word as the girls piled into the back of the yellow taxi and began their trip to the hotel. She just listened as Lexi babbled on about her latest date—some guy with a Ferrari who wanted to take her to his place in the Hamptons for a romantic weekend. But of course Lexi had said no. She didn't want to seem too interested, at least not until the second or third date.

Lexi droned on until the taxi pulled up in front of the Plaza's main entrance. She paid the driver, and the girls hopped out of the cab. Melanie and Lexi started up the steps. But Serena stayed behind.

Lexi looked back at Serena. The girl was frozen in place. Her left eye was blinking wildly, as though she had some nervous twitch that was beyond her control.

"What's the matter with her?" Lexi demanded of Melanie as she watched Serena twitch and blink. "Make her stop that. We can't go inside the Plaza with her eye doing weird things."

Melanie nodded. She walked over to Serena and put her arm around her shoulder. "You okay?" she asked as gently as she could. "It's not that big of a deal. We're just going to see if Eileen Kerr is here."

Serena rubbed at her eye. "Oh, I'm not nervous," she assured Melanie.

"Then what's with your eye?"

Serena giggled. "It's my contact lens, silly. It moved out of place. I'll fix it in a minute." She blinked her eye a few more times. "Ahh, that's better. Did my mascara run, Mel?"

Melanie surveyed her friend's face. "Nope. It's perfect," she assured her. "Sorry about that. We just figured you were—"

"You thought I was stressed or something. No, not me. I'm never afraid of meeting new people—not even really famous ones like Eileen Kerr. I figure she's just someone who's really good at what she does. But so am I. She's just better known."

Melanie smiled. What an awesome attitude. Serena was more laid-back about celebrities than any pseudo-blase New Yorker she'd ever met. New Yorkers always made it a point to walk past a star without looking them in the eye, as though they weren't at all excited to see them. But two minutes later they were bragging incessantly about the famous person they'd just spied. It was obvious that wasn't Serena's M.O. Maybe Serena was going to be okay to hang with after all.

"C'mon, Lexi," Serena said with a grin as she bounded past her on the Plaza steps. "We don't want to miss our opportunity."

"Will you look at her," Lexi moaned to Melanie. "She looks like a little pony, running like that. Once a farm girl, always a farm girl."

Melanie didn't reply. She was too busy trying to spot Eileen Kerr among the small groups of well-heeled people who were now milling in and out of the lobby of the Plaza Hotel. She'd seen only a few pictures of Eileen, a small, middle-aged woman with shoulder-length, chestnut brown hair that she usually wore pulled back in a business-like style. She only hoped she would recognize her tonight.

"Quick, let's get out of here," Serena whispered suddenly. "There's Ms. Geoffries."

Lexi and Melanie shifted their glances over to the far side of the lobby. Sure enough, there stood their headmistress, shaking hands with Eileen Kerr. Quickly, the girls darted around the corner and tried to shield their faces, pretending to look in the windows of the hotel shops.

"Is she gone yet?" Lexi whispered after a few long moments had gone by.

Melanie glanced out of the corner of her eye. "I don't see her."

Serena breathed a heavy sigh of relief. "That was close," she said.

"Why're y'all so afraid of that woman?" Lexi demanded. "We have just as much right to be here as she does. We don't have to be back at school for a few hours."

"Oh yeah? So how come you ran over here like a scared rat when we spotted her?" Melanie demanded. "Could it be that you didn't want her to know we were stalking Eileen Kerr?"

"We're not stalking her. We're just hoping to bump into her," Lexi corrected Melanie. She looked over at a pair of comfortable chairs where Eileen Kerr and a man were having a heated discussion. "And there she is, talking to one of her coaches."

"Let's go over and speak to her," Serena suggested.

Lexi shook her head. "I don't think so. I'm beginning to think that Melanie's right. It might actually seem like we were stalking her. Maybe we should change our plans, and talk to that coach instead. We'll wait until Eileen leaves, and then have a chat with him."

Melanie stared at the scented bracelet on Lexi's wrist. It was suddenly clear to her that this was no change in plans. Talking to a man was obviously what Lexi had had in mind from the very beginning.

After a few minutes, Eileen Kerr and her coach stood and shook hands. Eileen flashed the man a commanding smile and then headed for the elevator. The man didn't follow her. Instead, he turned and walked toward the door.

"I'm telling you that's the guy we want to talk to," Lexi told her friends. "He obviously has a lot of influence with Eileen Kerr. Let's follow him."

Melanie rolled her eyes. "Oh, but you're not a stalker or anything — right, Lexi?"

Lexi scowled, but didn't reply. Instead she ran her fingers through her hair and walked down the hotel steps and out into the street, being careful to remain just far enough from Eileen's coworker to avoid being noticed, but staying close enough so as not to lose him.

The girls followed the man into a small Mexican

eatery on Fifty-seventh Street. There was a bar area in the front of the restaurant. The man sat himself down at a cocktail table and waited for the waitress to serve him.

Lexi, Serena, and Melanie walked in only a few seconds behind him. The girls had to squint as their eyes adjusted to the smoke and dim lighting in the room. Serena rubbed her left eye. It was obvious the smoke was upsetting her contact lenses.

"Don't you dare start that blinking again!" Lexi ordered her.

Serena gulped. "I'll try."

"Good." Lexi's tone suddenly turned sticky sweet. "Look, this was my idea. There's always a chance he's gonna be really upset that we followed him here. If anyone is going to get the big brush-off, or get in trouble with Eileen Kerr, it should be me. Why don't you two go sit at the bar, and I'll find out if this guy is willing to talk to us."

From the moment Lexi sashayed over toward an empty seat on the other side of the coach's cocktail table, it was obvious she wasn't going to be calling Melanie and Serena over anytime soon. Within seconds she had made eye contact with her prey, and was already seducing him with her body language.

"Well, I guess Lexi has her own special way of communicating," Melanie growled under her breath.

"I don't think she's telling him about us," Serena agreed. "We may as well get out of here and head back. She can take a cab when she's ready to leave."

Melanie laughed. "My guess is Lexi won't be back at the school tonight. But don't worry, I'm sure she'll find a place to lay her head. 'Lay' being the operative word."

"So you wanna go?" Serena asked, trying to stifle a giggle. Lexi's sexual prowess was well-known at PCBS. She figured Melanie's assessment of the situation wasn't very far off base. Lexi would definitely have sex with this guy—especially if she thought it would secure her a spot in No Secrets. Lexi had slept with guys for a lot less important reasons than that.

Melanie nodded. "Okay. But do you mind if I have a diet Coke first? I'm dying of thirst."

"Sure," Serena agreed. "I'm kinda thirsty, too." She turned to the bartender. "One diet Coke and one iced tea, please."

"Coming right up, ladies." The bartender grinned, his bright white teeth shining through the dim light of the bar. He was tall and muscular, with a head of thick jet-black hair. Melanie figured he was either a model or an actor. Just like almost every bartender in New York City.

The bartender placed the drinks in front of Melanie and Serena. "That'll be eight dollars," he told them. "I'll run you a tab."

Melanie gasped as the bartender turned to serve a man at the other end of the bar. "Eight dollars for two soft drinks? That's a lot, even by Manhattan standards."

Serena took a sip of her iced tea and frowned. "Considering how lousy this tea is, it's robbery!" she declared as she took a huge gulp of her drink. "But I'll drink anything when I'm thirsty." She took another big sip.

"What do you mean it tastes lousy? Tea is tea," Melanie argued.

"I thought so, too. But this one just tastes really odd." Serena took another gulp and rolled up her shirtsleeves. "Is it my imagination, or is it getting really hot in here?"

Melanie shook her head. Glancing over toward Lexi, she commented, "The only thing that's hot in here is those two. Will you look at them?"

Serena looked over. Lexi was sitting practically nose to nose with the man they'd been following. She was casually rubbing her high-heeled foot up and down his calf, and laughing at everything he said. "Holy moley," Serena declared.

Melanie looked at her strangely. "Holy moley?"

Serena began to giggle uncontrollably. "It sounds pretty funny, doesn't it?" she agreed through her fits of laughter. She reached down and untucked her shirt from her skirt. She unbuttoned the bottom three buttons of her shirt and tied the ends in a knot above her belly button. "Sure is hot in here," she commented again as she took another sip of her iced tea.

Suddenly a loud chorus of shouting came from the far corner of the bar. A waitress, with a holster around her hips, placed a shot glass on the bar. She filled the glass with several kinds of liquor and banged it on the table. The drink began to fizz.

"Slammer! Slammer!" the group of guys who had ordered the drink began chanting as one of them chugged down the drink.

"Whoa! Check that out!" Serena exclaimed in an unusually loud voice. "I wish we could try one."

"They'd never serve us alcohol in this place," Melanie assured her. "We're underage. I'm surprised they're even letting us sit here at the bar."

"Yeah, but would they let us sit on the bar?" Serena asked in the rowdiest voice Melanie had ever heard emanate from her lips. Instantly Serena hopped up on top of the bar and took another sip of her tea.

Melanie was worried now. Serena was acting pretty wild—especially for her. If she didn't know better . . . Melanie's mind began to race. Serena had ordered an iced tea. What if the bartender had given her a Long Island Iced Tea—one that was made with alcohol? Quickly, Melanie sniffed at Serena's glass. It smelled of booze big time. No wonder Serena had thought the drink tasted strange. She'd probably never had liquor before in her life. And now she'd had half a glass of one of the strongest drinks imaginable. Serena was drunk. Melanie had to get her out of the bar before she got into trouble.

But Melanie didn't act quickly enough. Before she could drop eight dollars on the counter and grab Serena, the country girl stood up on the bar and began shouting over the crowd, "Slammer! Slammer! Slammer!"

The bartender came running over. "You'd better

get your friend out of here," he ordered Melanie. "This is a nice bar. It's not something out of Coyote Ugly. We don't need girls like that around here."

Melanie was fuming now. Serena's behavior was his fault, after all. "Maybe you should've thought of that before you served a sixteen-year-old a Long Island Iced Tea. All she wanted was some cold Liptons, you jerk!"

"Aw jeez," the bartender gulped as his face turned beet red. "She's underage? I could lose my job for this. Look, the drinks are on me, okay? Just get her out of here before my boss finds out."

Melanie put her eight dollars back in her pocket and yanked Serena off the bar.

"Where're we goin'?" Serena mumbled as she followed Melanie toward the door.

"Back to the school," Melanie replied.

"Okeydokey," Serena said, giggling. Then she turned toward Lexi. At the top of her lungs she shouted toward her schoolmate, "We're goin' back now, Lexi. Have fun!"

The last thing Serena saw as she left the bar was Lexi and the coach laughing in her direction.

Self-Expression Journal

This is so embarrassing. I can hardly believe I'm writing this in my journal. But we're supposed to talk about anything that is really meanngful in our lives, and I think the first time you get drunk is kinda meaningful. And that's what happened to me last night——apparently.

My head hurts so bad this morning. Melanie spent the night in my room, making sure that I threw up in a bucket when the room started spinning around. It seemed like every time I closed my eyes the bed began moving in circles.

In my whole life I've never heard of a Long Island Iced Tea. But you can bet that from now on, I'll order nothing but bottled water or club soda. I'm not taking the chance of being misunderstood like that again.

I can't believe I actually stood up on the bar. That's not my style at all. Nobody back home would ever believe that I did that. Not that I'm planning on telling anybody at home what happened last night. The fewer people who know, the better.

Unfortunately, one of the people who did witness my performance last night was that coach from Omega Talent. I can only imagine what he must think of me now. I guess I can kiss my chances of being a No Secrets finalist good-bye now. The last thing Eileen Kerr would want in her band is an underage, booze-drinking party girl. And I'm pretty sure that's what that coach thought I was.

The thing that's so frustrating is that it wasn't even my fault. I wish I could sue that bartender for destroying my career, but I don't even know his name. And I have a feeling that even if I went back to the bar to find him, I'd never remember what he looked like. I don't remember a whole lot of details from last night. I mean, I remember most of the major, incredibly embarrassing stuff, but a lot of the details are lost. Like Melanie says when we left the bar I wanted to go back to the Plaza and dance in the fountain outside the hotel. I don't remember that at all! I was so lucky to have Melanie with me last night. She really knew what to do with me—especially when I got sick. She made me feel so much better.

Too bad Melanie can't fix my biggest problem, though. Nothing she or anyone else can do is gonna get me into No Secrets. But I have to put that out of my head right now. I've got to just focus on the showcase. I'm supposed to meet Katie and Alyssa in the piano lab to go over our big number for the show. I'm not looking forward to trying to sing jazz with this headache. But I can't let them down, so I'm just going to have to muddle through the best I can. The show must go on.

I think I've learned my lesson the hard way. From now on, I'm staying out of Lexi's schemes. If I ever decide to listen to her again, I hope somebody will tie me up and lock me in my room so I can't go. That girl is dangerous.

She's also probably in plenty of trouble. It's ten o'clock in the morning, and she's still not back. I can just see her trying to hail a cab today. That fancy black dress is going to look mighty strange in the daytime.

I think I'm going to take another aspirin now. It's nice to have someplace where I can reveal my biggest secrets. I'll write again soon.

Luv,
Serena

Chapter 7

"Five, six, seven, eight!" Alyssa stretched her leg long, turned, and leaned seductively over the side of the piano. "A fine romance," she sang out, making her voice slightly gravelly, like Billie Holiday used to sound. "A fine romance." Alyssa sang a few more words and then looked at Katie. "That's where you're supposed to come in," she reminded her.

"Sorry," Katie apologized. "I missed the cue."

"You've been missing cues all morning. You both have. What's the problem?"

Serena rolled her eyes. "I just feel lousy," she said. "All I want to do is sleep."

Alyssa sighed. Illness was one of the few things that was out of her control. And Alyssa hated when things were out of her control. "Okay. So what's up with you, Katie?"

Katie shrugged. "Nothing. I just got another letter from Keith, that's all."

Alyssa put her hands on her hips and looked at Katie with a slightly annoyed stare. "Why do you stick with this guy?" she demanded. "All he does is bring you down."

"Not all the time," Katie assured her. "Y'all just don't know him the way I do. Sometimes he can be sweet, and kind, and loving." The trouble was, he hadn't been any of those things lately. All he'd been was discouraging and demanding. And still, Katie loved him. She always had—from that first day in the fifth grade when she'd seen him in the cafeteria, eating his dessert before his hot dog. She'd thought that was so daring and cool. Katie couldn't remember a time when Keith hadn't been part of her life. She wasn't totally sure she could make it without him now.

"Well look, we're not getting anywhere today," Alyssa told the others. "Serena, you look like crap. And Katie . . ." Her voice drifted away with unspoken disappointment.

"You're right, 'Lyss," Katie agreed. "I'll be better tomorrow. You know what? I'm going to pick up those sparkly feather boas I saw at Alice's Looking Glass— y' know, that little thrift shop on Bleecker Street. They'd be great for this number. I could use a little mindless shopping today. And that way we'd be able to rehearse with the boas tomorrow."

Alyssa took off her jazz shoes and wiggled her bare toes. "You guys go ahead," she told Katie and Serena. "I'll lock up."

Katie liked the feel of the cool fall breeze hitting her across the face as she walked from the Eighth Street subway stop toward Bleecker Street. She smiled at a group of NYU students who were dressed in total Goth-wear—black fishnet stockings with tears in them, over-dyed straight black hair, long dark trench coats, and giant, rhinestone-encrusted crucifixes. Now that was something you wouldn't see every day in Texas!

Katie could practically hear Keith's reaction to her thoughts: "Why would you want to see people dressed like that?" he would be certain to ask. Katie closed her eyes and shook her head, trying to knock any thoughts of Keith out of her mind. She wasn't going to think about her problems now. She was just going to shop. What was it Susie always liked to say? Oh yeah: "When the going gets tough, the tough go shopping."

Katie stopped outside an ear-piercing stand at the corner of Broadway and Waverly Street. She watched through the window as a guy who looked about eighteen got his tongue pierced by a heavyset man with a series of tattoos going up and down his arm. For a moment, Katie thought about getting her belly button pierced. She'd always wanted to do something a little radical, and a piercing just didn't seem as permanent an act as getting a tattoo.

"Don't do it."

A deep voice interrupted Katie's thoughts. She turned quickly to see a man of about thirty, with slightly receding, curly, sandy-brown hair and big hazel eyes, staring at her.

"Don't do what?" Katie asked him.

"Don't pierce anything. You're perfect just the way

you are right now."

Katie blushed, and fidgeted with the collar of her gray and burgundy cardigan. "I really wasn't going to—"

"Oh and you have a southern accent, too," the man interrupted her. "Where are you from? Atlanta?"

Katie shook her head. "Texas."

"Oh, a Dallas girl, like the Ewings of South Fork."

"Outside of Houston, actually," Katie informed him, choking back a laugh. New Yorkers were so funny. When it came to anything outside of their city they always seemed to think in terms of things they'd seen on TV. This guy wasn't the first one to assume that all Texans lived on big ranches and owned about a dozen high-producing oil wells like the characters on that old TV show, *Dallas*.

The man studied Katie's brown cowboy boots. Then he allowed his eye to slowly drift up her long legs and trace her body until his eyes met hers. "You're absolutely amazing."

Katie looked at the man with skepticism. "I am?"

"You sure are," he assured her. He held out his hand. "I'm Lucas Harriman."

Katie shook his hand quickly. "Katie Marr."

Lucas smiled. "Would you like to go for a coffee, Katie Marr?" he asked.

Now Katie was getting nervous. This guy was definitely too old to be picking up teenagers in the Village.

"Uh, no thanks," Katie replied quickly. She turned toward Bleecker Street. "I've got some errands to run.

So—"

Lucas laughed. "Oh, it's not what you think," he assured her. "I'm a photographer. And I think you'd make a wonderful fashion model."

Katie shook her head. Now there was a line straight out of a bad movie. "I don't think so," she answered him.

Lucas reached into his pocket and pulled out a small white business card. He handed it to Katie. "This should prove that I'm legit," he told her patiently.

Katie turned the card over. It read:

LUCAS HARRIMAN
PHOTOGRAPHER
STARLIGHT STUDIOS
(212) 555-8333

Katie smiled. "Okay, so you're legit. But I still have to go."

Lucas nodded. "Look, I think you could really have a career in this. I have to do a fashion spread for a national magazine. I was going to go through one of the agencies, but I'd much rather know that I had a part in launching a new career." He studied Katie's dubious expression. "How about you think it over? If you decide you want to give modeling a try, give me a call—but try to decide ASAP. I have to start shooting Monday afternoon."

Katie pocketed the card. "Okay, I'll think about it."

Lucas grinned. "That's all I ask," he responded. Then he turned and headed toward Washington

Square Park. "I'm not kidding, Katie. An all-American type like you could become huge in the magazine world. *Huge*."

Katie took a deep breath. This was beginning to sound very exciting. But she didn't want to let on that she was as thrilled as she really felt. "See ya," she remarked cheerily as she headed for Bleecker Street. As she walked down the street Katie prayed that Lucas Harriman couldn't tell that she was so excited, her legs felt like Jell-O.

As soon as Katie returned to PCBS she raced to the seventh-floor hall phone. Quickly she pulled out her phone card and dialed Keith's number.

"Hello?"

Katie was surprised that Keith's slow, southern drawl could still make her melt—even from thousands of miles away. Whenever she talked to him she could feel herself longing to be near him—to smell his cologne, and feel his strong arm around her shoulders. "Keith, it's me," she said finally.

"Hi, sugar," he greeted Katie.

"Keith, you are never going to believe this!" she shouted into the phone.

"You're coming home?" he asked excitedly.

"No, not till Thanksgiving," she told him softly. "This is about my career. Today I was in the Village, y'know, just walking down the street, and this older man comes up to me and—"

"How much older?" Keith interrupted.

"Oh, he was at least thirty," Katie assured him. "Relax, it was nothing like that. He was a professional photographer, and he wants me to model for a national magazine. Can you imagine, Keith? All those people walking down the street, and he spots me!"

Keith snickered. "Oh, I can imagine it, sug. He probably spotted how naive you are compared with the other people in Greenwich Village. I'll bet this old dude wants to do a lot more than take your picture. You'd better not go up to that studio. Something awful might happen."

Katie couldn't believe it. She'd thought Keith would be happy that she actually had a shot at making it in modeling in New York City. She assumed he'd be happy that all of his fears about her having to face rejection were for nothing. But instead he was knocking her dreams—and making her feel like a fool.

At first Katie couldn't answer Keith. The words seemed stuck in her throat. Finally she took a deep breath and forced them out. "I don't believe you!" she shouted angrily into the phone. "This guy is legit. Why can't you just accept the fact that someone who is a professional thinks I have what it takes to be a model?"

"Oh, come on, Katie," Keith said. "You know I think you're gorgeous. But I'm in love with you."

"So no one else can find me attractive without wanting to sleep with me?" Katie demanded.

"I didn't say that," Keith replied. "But you have to admit—"

"I don't have to admit anything," Katie told him.

"Up until this minute I wasn't even sure if I was going to agree to do the shoot—I should be concentrating on the showcase. But now, I'm going to call up and tell Lucas Harriman that I'll be his newest modeling discovery—just to prove to you that I have what it takes."

"You'd better not," Keith ordered, his voice growing more menacing now. "You're gonna get yourself into some major trouble. And this time I won't be there to get you out of it."

Katie slammed the receiver, hard. Then she reached into her jeans pocket and pulled out Lucas Harriman's business card. Without taking any time to think, she dialed the phone number on the card. "Hello, Lucas," she said boldly. "It's Katie Marr. What time would you like me to come to your studio on Monday?"

Chapter 8

Sunday mornings were usually quiet at PCBS, but this Sunday the rehearsal rooms, dance studios, and stages were filled with girls practicing their showcase performance pieces. Ever since Ms. Geoffries had announced that Eileen Kerr and her team of coaches would be milling around the school searching for a few dedicated performers, everyone had been working twice as hard as they normally would. Not only were the girls determined to make this a showcase to remember—they also wanted to show Eileen Kerr that they could completely dedicate themselves to a project.

Well, almost everyone felt that way. Melanie was not particularly interested in what Eileen Kerr thought about her. She already knew she wasn't Omega Talent material. So when Cass asked Hannah and Melanie if they could work up an even more complicated dance number, Mel had balked at the idea. She had no reason to put in the extra effort. She wasn't interested in impressing Eileen Kerr.

Meet the girls!

Cass

Alyssa

Daria

Hannah

Janine

Katie

Lexi

Melanie

Serena

Susie

Alyssa shares the good news: Eileen Kerr is coming to the Professional Children's Boarding School to search for the members of her new band, No Secrets!

Katie can't stop worrying about her boyfriend, Keith, back home in Texas.

Hannah talks to her mother on a pay phone. She can't let anyone know the truth about her life.

Melanie and Serena don't know that Lexi has her own plans for securing her spot in No Secrets.

Dress rehearsal for the Fall Showcase is even more important than usual—everyone knows Eileen Kerr will be in the audience!

Lexi can't believe that a tabloid reporter has ruined her plans and her reputation! Now she's lost her chance to be in No Secrets!

Eileen Kerr chooses the eight lucky finalists for No Secrets. Each is closer to her dream of becoming a star!

"Cass, the song has a simple message: Listen to your children, they have something to say. Why complicate it with intricate dance moves just to prove that we can dance better than someone else?"

"I think Cass is right, Melanie," Hannah interjected in her calm, cool voice. "A lot of the adults in the audience might be uncomfortable with the theme of the song, and the dancing will sort of, you know, distract them."

Melanie looked as though she wanted to choke Hannah. She'd worked long and hard to write that song. "I don't want them to be distracted. I want them to listen to the words." She paused and sneered in Hannah's direction. "I guess some of us don't have to rebel against our picture-perfect lives. But then again, if you've never suffered, I guess you don't know what it's like to have something to say."

Hannah reddened. She'd suffered plenty. More than Melanie knew; more than she'd ever know. But Hannah would never give her the satisfaction of letting her in on the truth.

Cass smoothly inched her body between the two feuding girls. "Hannah, I think what Melanie is saying is that each generation of teens has felt ignored, because that's what always happens. Then everybody vows they'll be different from their parents, and then winds up becoming pretty much the same."

All three girls went silent at that idea. Each was making a silent, sacred promise to themselves not to let that be their own fate.

"Besides, I think Melanie's hard-edged rock-rap-pop fusion sound makes the message totally fresh," Cass continued. She turned to Melanie. "That's why I want to make the dance number even more intense. I want to make your song part of a performance piece they'll never forget!"

Melanie nodded. It was hard to argue with Cassidy when she got into her UN diplomacy mode. "All right, Cass. You win," she agreed.

Cass demonstrated a few of the ideas she had for spicing up the dance number. Before long, all three girls were dancing to a recorded version of Melanie's song. The recording had the words and the music in place. Of course at the real performance, the girls would be singing and dancing while a hired pianist accompanied them.

Cass, Melanie, and Hannah were so caught up in the concentration that came from trying to memorize intricate arm, leg, and head movements that they never heard the strong knock on the door.

When no response came to her knocking, a tall, bleached-blond woman with large sunglasses and a long faux-fur coat swept her way uninvited into the rehearsal hall. "Cassy!" she cried out excitedly.

Cass stopped in midstep and stared at the woman with surprise. "Mom?" she asked nervously. "What're you doing here?"

"I caught the first flight out of LAX as soon as I heard, darling."

"Heard about what?" Cass asked suspiciously.

"About Eileen Kerr, of course, you silly. It's been in all the trades!"

Cass sighed. Her mother continued to read the show business trade papers, even though Cass hadn't had a professional job in two years. Oh well, Cass mused, once your daughter's agent, always your daughter's agent. "What does Eileen Kerr's visit have to do with you, Mother?" Cass asked her finally.

"Oh, I'm just here for moral support." She turned to Melanie and Hannah. "Hi, girls. I'm Alana Morgan."

Melanie looked at Cass with confusion.

"She uses her maiden name since the divorce," Cass explained to her friends. She smiled at her mother and began to introduce her. "This is Melanie, and Hannah. Look, Mom, we're kinda in the middle of a rehearsal here and—"

"I know. I was watching from the doorway. That's quite an original piece you're working on."

Melanie bit her lip to keep from barking out that the song was obviously written for uptight adults like Alana Morgan, and that naturally she wouldn't get it. But the woman was Cass's mom, and Melanie didn't want to start anything.

"How about I meet you at the hotel, Mom?" Cass suggested hurriedly.

"Look Cass, I'm wiped," Hannah told her. "And I still have to study for that chem test. Why don't we quit now, and we can work on this some more after dinner tonight."

Melanie nodded. "I'm writing a new song for

65

composition class, and I think there's a totally fresh idea coming on. You go ahead, Cass."

Cass shrugged. "I guess you win then, Mom. Just let me shower and clean up. I'll meet you in the lobby in ten minutes."

Alana laughed. "Oh Cassie, don't be absurd," she told her. "I'll wait in your room. I can't wait to see what you've done with some of those posters I sent you."

Cass rolled her eyes. Her mother wouldn't have been at all thrilled with what Cass had done with those tacky Hollywood movie premiere posters Alana had sent—unless of course she'd meant for them to wind up in the garbage.

But Cass didn't argue. "All right, Mom," she acquiesced as always. "Whatever you think is best."

Serena looked up as Lexi spilled into the dorm room the two girls shared, and kicked off her stilletto heels. "Your mom called again," Serena mentioned without even looking up.

"What'd you tell her?" Lexi asked as she opened her closet door and began looking for a more comfortable pair of shoes.

"Just what you told me to tell her—that you were at the library . . . again."

Lexi flashed Serena one of her sticky-sweet condescending smiles. "That's great, darlin'," she thanked her. "I owe ya one."

Serena shook her head. "You owe me more than that. I don't like lying to your mom—especially when

I don't even know the truth. Where have you been sneaking off to, Lexi?"

Lexi looked Serena in the eye. "You don't want to get involved, Serena. Believe me, it's better this way," she assured her roommate. "Now do me a little favor, willya? Next time my mom calls, tell her I'm taking a dance class. We've got to vary the excuses a little bit."

As Lexi dashed out of the room, yet again, Serena let out a huge sigh. "We?" she asked aloud. "Since when is this my problem?"

Cass and her mom sat in the small Cajun café and looked at the menu. "Blue Bayou, what a funny name for a restaurant," Alana mused as she looked disdainfully at the cafe's pseudo-New Orleans style decor. "Is this the new in-spot for performers?"

Cass shook her head. "It's just a place where I like the food. I'm not usually into celeb sightings."

Alana lowered her sunglasses and stared into her daughter's eyes. "Darling, it's not a matter of seeing; it's a matter of being seen. I'm sure there are plenty of people in the biz who still remember what a talented performer you are — even though two years is a long time to be across the continent from Hollywood."

"Mom, New York has a whole professional community, too," Cass reminded her. "And I kinda like that there are plenty of people here who don't care about show business at all."

Alana shook her head. "You'll never get back on TV with an attitude like that," she reproached her daughter. "Then again, if Eileen Kerr chooses you to be one of the members of her new group, you won't need TV—at least not for a while."

Cass rolled her eyes, but didn't respond. Some things never changed.

"Which leads me to an important issue," Alana continued, not noticing her daughter's exhausted expression. "Those two girls you were rehearsing with today have got to go."

"Melanie and Hannah? Why?" Cass asked as she took a huge gulp of her lemon water.

"Oh darling, you have got to be kidding. It's so obvious that you were assigned to their group to make them look good. And frankly, that's not your job. Now I'll just go and have a talk with Ms. Geoffries, and tell her that you'd rather perform alone and—"

"I wasn't assigned to them. I wanted to work with them. I think they're talented. Did you know Melanie wrote 'Open the Lines' herself?"

"I can tell!" Alana barked, her voice registering frustration and a decided lack of patience. "Please, that song is so amateurish. Angry teen rantings went out with the Seattle sound. And her look is just so edgy. Can you imagine Eileen Kerr choosing Melanie for her group? She'd probably be afraid to run into her on the street, never mind travel with her on the road. You know what they say, dear: You're judged by the company you keep.

"And that Hannah," Alana continued, barely stopping to take a breath. "She's obviously more into having the right ensemble than into working on her dancing and voice projection. Of course, having a flair for fashion probably helps her cover for her marked lack of talent."

Cass took a small bite of her blackened catfish and chewed hard. She'd learned long ago not to argue with her mother when she got like this. It was pointless.

"Now I think we need to find a number that can show how versatile your singing voice is," Alana suggested eagerly. "Not something as young as the songs you sang on *The Kids Company*, but a solo that's still happy and upbeat—maybe something about a teenager in love. Well, that doesn't matter right now. I'm sure Kenny can help us find the perfect tune for your voice."

Cass sighed. Kenny Miller had been the musical director on *The Kids Company*. Alana always found a reason to meet up with him when she found herself waxing nostalgic for the good old days, back when she'd been Cass's chaperon on the set of the show. Alana and Kenny had become good friends back then—very good friends. But their relationship had ended shortly after the show did. Cass was not surprised her mother wanted to renew her contact with him now.

"Mom, will you excuse me?" Cass asked. "I need to go to the ladies' room. I'll be back in a moment."

Alana smiled. "Of course, dear. And while you're gone, I'll jot down a few notes about how we might want to restyle your hair, and what kind of outfit we can put together. Oh sweetie, this is going to be such fun—just like the old days."

Cass forced herself to smile and then hurried into the ladies' room. After checking that no one else was in there with her, Cass quickly dashed into one of the stalls and promptly made herself throw up.

By the time Cassidy got back to the school, she was worn out from listening to her mother. The last thing she wanted was a confrontation with Melanie and Hannah—at least not until she'd figured out a way to break the news to them that she was going to be doing her own piece for the showcase. So she was less than thrilled when the two girls knocked on her door shortly after seven o'clock.

"We missed you at dinner," Melanie greeted Cass.

"I ate so much with my mom, I think I'll be full for a week," Cass told her.

"Okay, so then you wanna work on the number now?" Melanie asked.

"Well, about the number . . . ," Cass began nervously.

"I know, we were a little shaky on synchronizing those turns," Hannah interrupted.

Cass shook her head. "That's not it. The turns are fine. It's just that, well, I don't think I'm the right person to . . ."

Cass didn't have to say another thing. Melanie got her drift right away. "It's just that your mother doesn't think we're good enough for you—right, Cass?"

Cass didn't say a word. It sounded so awful when Melanie put it that way. It wasn't like that. Alana just seemed to have a good eye for knowing what was right for her daughter. Cass had come to depend on her for that. "Look, you guys could do it as a duet. It would work better that way," Cass said, trying as always not to hurt anyone's feelings—or to let anyone down. "I come with a lot of baggage, Mel. When people think of me, they remember all that *Kids Company* 'family entertainment' junk. I don't have the right image for your song."

Hannah stared angrily into Cass's pained eyes. "Let me get this straight. You want me to work with her—without you?"

Melanie moaned. "I'm not so thrilled about the idea either, princess. I wouldn't be working with you at all if Cass hadn't convinced me that we harmonize well together."

"And you do," Cass leaped in, before Hannah could snap back. "Beautifully. You'll be great in the showcase."

Hannah turned her back on Cass. There was nothing more to say.

"Fine, Cass," Melanie said. "We'll go it alone. I'm sure you and your momma will find just the right song to keep your reputation intact."

Cass fought the tears in her eyes as Melanie and Hannah walked away. She knew that her mother's advice was the best thing for her. She only wished it didn't hurt so much.

Self-Expression Journal Entry

I know I should be really pissed off at Cass for dumping me the way she did tonight, but I just can't be. I mean, I thought I had it rough with my mom never being there for me when I was a kid, but I actually think Cass has it worse. She can't breathe without getting permission from her mother—and I really think that woman is slowly suffocating her.

I know that one of the things Cass liked about being at this school was that she was so far away from her mother. Sure, she got snail mail, e-mail, and phone calls from her, but at least she was free from the dragon lady's stranglehold most of the time. Cass could make her own decisions . . . at least about some things. And I think she enjoyed doing that.

But I can't worry too much about Cass now. I've got my own problems. You can't imagine how awful it was being alone in that rehearsal hall tonight with Her Highness, Princess Hannah of Snootville! I hate the way she looks at me— y'know, kinda staring down from the tip of her nose, like just cuz she's got money, she's better than I am.

Give me a break. Sooner or later she's gonna learn that when we're on that stage we're gonna be judged on what we can do, not what we can buy! I mean, her fancy jazz shoes don't make her dance better than I do. And all the fancy voice lessons in the world can't make her singing ring true—like it's coming from her soul. She's got the rhythm down, and the notes are right, but there's something missing. It's like it's all an illusion with no real substance.

On the other hand, I'm not complaining. At least she's willing to work hard on the song. I even think she's kinda getting to like my music. And she's agreed to keep all the new dance moves we worked up with Cass in the routine. Thank God! I'd totally lose it if I had to start from scratch at this point. I mean, I know I'm not going to be one of Eileen Kerr's little No Secrets Barbie dolls, but I do want to make a good showing at the performance. This is the first time a real audience is going to hear my music. That's a big deal. It's like I'm sharing a little bit of myself with them. And what they think is really gonna matter.

So I guess I'm glad Hannah is willing to work with me on this. Which is more than I can say for Cass. But like I said, I don't really blame Cass. She's all caught up in this control thing with her mother.

But hey, not my problem.

Catch ya later,

Melanie

Chapter 9

"I just don't know how much of this I can take, 'Lyss," Janine moaned as she flopped down on Alyssa's bed late Monday afternoon. "Daria's a total dictator. "

Susie nodded in agreement. "She's decided that we're going to be her backup singers. It's like we're the Supremes and she's Diana Ross or something."

Alyssa laughed. "Well, it's better than being two Pips while she's Gladys Knight."

"Or she's Michael, and we're the other, nameless Jackson brothers," Susie countered.

Janine moaned. "Enough with the Motown catalog, you guys. This is no joke. With her at center stage, who's going to notice us?"

Alyssa sighed. "Now, I'm not one to say, 'I told you so' . . ."

"Since when?" Janine interrupted her.

Alyssa had to laugh. She was actually one to gloat now and again. But she resisted the urge this time. "Look, why do you two put up with her garbage? Just say no."

"That's easier said than done," Susie moaned. "You know how Daria is. If you cross her, she just gets so . . . so . . . so—"

"Mean?" Alyssa suggested. "Vicious? Rotten? Evil?"

Janine laughed in spite of herself. "All of the above."

"Well, if you ask me, you guys have two choices: You stay on Daria's good side—whatever good side she has—and give up your shot at being in No Secrets, or you can tell Daria to shove it, and give Eileen Kerr a performance she has to notice," Alyssa suggested.

Janine shook her head. "You make it sound so simple."

"It is," Alyssa assured her.

"We'll work on the bravery thing," Susie vowed. She brushed her blond bangs from her eyes and sat up. Her eyes practically glowed as she got ready to dish some hot dirt. "Not to change the subject or anything, but have you guys seen Lexi lately?"

Janine thought for a moment. "Y'know, come to think of it, she hasn't really been around much. I'll bet her dance partners are pretty angry with her. Hey, who is she performing with, anyway?"

Susie shook her head. "That's just it. She doesn't have any partners. She dropped out of her dance number over the weekend. J. C., one of the girls in her group, said she told them that she was just going to be in the big production numbers."

"Why?" Janine asked.

Susie shrugged. "Who knows? But yesterday I asked Lexi if she was rehearsing at some professional studio space, since she's never around here, and she said the strangest thing."

"What?" Alyssa demanded.

"She said she's been busy working on getting herself chosen for No Secrets, but that she didn't need to do any rehearsing to do it. She made it sound like she had it in the bag already."

Janine laughed. "Maybe some boyfriend with a Ferrari is going to buy her a spot in the band."

"Fat chance," Alyssa assured her. "Eileen Kerr doesn't need the money. What she needs is a talented group of girls."

"Well, I do think Lexi's spending a lot of her time with a guy, though," Susie told the others. "She's been putting on the perfume pretty heavily. And every time I see her, she's dressed in all these totally hot outfits—y'know, those dresses where the back plunges down to your butt, and the slit on the side goes up to your waist."

"That girl can be such a hoochie," Janine agreed with a sigh. "Look, I'm sick of talking about Lexi's love life. She's gone through at least six heavy romances since I've been at this school, and I can't even manage to get one little date. Just thinking about it gets me depressed."

Alyssa and Susie nodded in agreement. Their love lives weren't exactly the stuff romance novels were made of, either.

Susie turned to Alyssa. "How's your showcase number coming along?" she asked, in yet another attempt to change the subject. "Are you whipping Serena and Katie into tip-top shape, Sergeant?"

Alyssa smiled at Katie's nickname for her. If she only knew what real boot camp was like! "Oh, our song's okay, I guess," Alyssa replied with just a touch of doubt in her usually positive tone. "Serena's been putting in a lot of effort, but Katie's been kinda distracted since last week. I think Keith's been bugging her to come home again. You know how she gets whenever he plays the guilt card with her."

"Anyway, we were s'posed to rehearse today, but Katie told us she had some appointment to keep in the Village. We really need to rehearse, though. All I can say is that it better have been an important meeting."

Katie stood outside the West Village brownstone for a few minutes and tried to stop her heart from pounding with excitement. But she couldn't hold back the thrills. She was about to experience her very first professional gig, modeling for a magazine in New York City! Other girls just dreamed of opportunities like this, and here she was about to experience it. This was amazing!

But Katie really wanted to seem like a professional when she entered that studio for the first time. And somehow she didn't think Tyra Banks, Cindy Crawford, or Kate Moss were so nervous when they went on a shoot that they couldn't catch their breath.

But hard as she tried, there was no way Katie

could act blasé about this. It was just too big! In the end, she decided to just go up to Luke's studio and be herself. After all, he knew she wasn't an experienced model—and he still thought she'd be perfect for the shoot, didn't he? Without taking another minute to think, she pressed the studio bell and waited for Luke to buzz her in.

It was four long flights of stairs to the top floor of the building, where Luke's studio was located. But Katie barely felt her feet touch the stairs as she practically flew upward. When she reached the top, Luke was standing by an open doorway. He flashed Katie a charming smile as she reached the landing.

"Well, you don't have to do the StairMaster today, kiddo," he greeted her. "You've just completed my own personal workout routine."

"At least it's cheaper than joining a gym," Katie laughed, trying to sound confident and grown up.

"A girl with your body obviously works out a lot," Lucas noted, looking her up and down with a knowledgeable eye.

Katie blushed. No man—other than Keith of course—had ever looked at her in quite that way.

"Okay, so let's get started. I've got the contracts and release forms right here—unless of course you want me to go through your agent."

Katie shook her head. "I don't have an agent."

Lucas smiled in a way that made Katie think he already knew that. "Well, then, how old are you?" Lucas asked bluntly.

Katie thought for a moment. If he knew that she was only seventeen, he might have to get her to send the forms to her parents for their signature, which could take a while, or worse yet, call off the whole deal right then and there. "I turned eighteen in March," she lied quickly.

"Well, all right, then," Lucas replied. He handed her a stack of forms. "I've placed an X next to each place you're supposed to sign. You don't need to read all the fine print. That'll take forever, and it's all the usual legalese. They're standard forms. Basically it just says I'll pay you one thousand dollars for your work today, and then I own the rights to the pictures. It should take about three hours or so to finish the shoot. Does that sound reasonable to you?"

Katie gasped audibly. A thousand dollars for three hours' work? Yikes! It was almost too good to be true.

But it was true. She really was here in a photographer's studio. The lights were set up, and the white paper backdrop was in place. Already she was getting big money for her work. Quickly she picked up her pen and began to sign the forms. When she was finished, she handed the pen to Lucas. "There!" she announced with a great flourish.

"Great," Lucas replied. He pointed toward a small room off to the side of his studio. "You'll find your outfits in there. We're gonna shoot in order, starting with the silver and cranberry one."

Katie smiled and walked into the dressing room. What she found there completely blew her mind. Laid out on a table were four different thong bathing suits. Some had tiny bikini tops, and some just appeared to be thongs with no tops at all. She scouted around quickly for bathing suit cover-ups, or robes or something. But there were no other clothes anywhere in the room.

And that's when it hit her. No wonder Lucas had made it a point to tell her she didn't have to read the fine print on those contracts. It would've had a clause about nudity, for sure. And the reason he was paying her so much money was to buy the rights to the pictures outright. She'd never have any control over where he used them.

Suddenly Katie wasn't so sure this photo shoot was legit. There was a distinct possibility that Lucas was just some perv trying to get a free peek show! And even if it was a legitimate photo session for a real magazine, it wasn't a mag Katie would ever want to be seen in! Suddenly she had a horrible image of her picture appearing on the walls of car repair shops and guys' dorm rooms across the country. The thought of being the object of their sick fantasies made her physically ill! Frantically she forced open the dressing room door and ran for the stairway.

"Where are you going?" Lucas called after her in surprise. "We had a deal. You signed the contracts. Look baby, you get back here right now or your name will mean nothing in the modeling world! Nobody wants to work with a girl who's afraid to show a little skin. That's what sells!"

Katie was crying now. She could feel the tears streaming down her face as she ran. She wanted to turn around and scream—to let all of her pain, anger, and shame out through her lungs. But she just couldn't manage to get the words out. So she kept running. Even when she was out on the street, and a cold, icy rain began to fall, Katie kept running—faster, and faster until she could think of nothing but the shortness of her breath.

"What're you doing?" Alyssa asked as she walked into Katie's room late in the afternoon. Katie jumped with surprise, then quickly hid her face so Alyssa couldn't see her tears. The last thing she wanted right now was to have to tell her friend what a complete jerk she'd been. "I don't want to talk about it," she mumbled. "I kinda want to be alone right now, Alyssa."

Alyssa peered over Katie's shoulder. She saw a half-packed suitcase lying on the bed. "It looks like you're packing," Alyssa continued, refusing to leave. "Are you getting ready for Thanksgiving break a few days early?"

Katie shook her head. "I'm going home . . . for good," she replied simply.

The shock registered on Alyssa's face. "Are you nuts?" she exclaimed. "You're leaving the school three days before the showcase?"

Katie stopped packing. The showcase. She'd totally forgotten about the showcase. Alyssa and Serena were going to be plenty mad at her for leaving now. But they'd deal. They were almost professional now. They would find a way to make the piece work without her.

"I'm sorry about that, Alyssa. But I can't stay here anymore. I know y'all will hate me forever for cuttin' out on the number in the showcase, but . . ." Her voice choked before she could finish the sentence.

Alyssa's eyes filled with anger—but not at Katie. "Is this about Keith? Did he write you another letter? Or call you?"

Katie shook her head. "This isn't about Keith," she assured her. "He's a really sweet guy, Alyssa. I know everybody thinks he's some sort of controlling jerk, but y'all don't know him like I do. I wish y'all could meet him. Then you'd understand that he was just trying to protect me from . . . from . . ."

"From what?" Alyssa demanded. "From living your dream? From performing for thousands of people? From being everything you can be?"

Katie shook her head. "No. He's tryin' to protect me from sick photographers, and directors, and casting people who are only interested in one thing, and who use you and abuse you, and then throw you out when you're not worth anything to them anymore."

Alyssa was confused. "What're you talking about?" she asked.

Katie took a deep breath. "All I can say, Alyssa, is if you're smart, you'll listen to your dad and just go back to the base. Take a safe job where you can still be creative, but you can't be hurt."

Alyssa eyed Katie curiously. "What happened this afternoon, Katie?" she asked. "You can tell me."

Katie couldn't hold it in any longer. As the tears poured out of her she practically vomited the whole nasty story about Lucas—how she'd been fooled into believing she really had something special, and how he'd taken advantage of her need to feel like she really could make it in New York.

Alyssa listened without making a comment. She sensed instinctively that Katie had to tell the entire story in order to let the whole thing go. When she knew for sure that Katie had nothing more to say, Alyssa held her close and let her cry. "Hey, it's okay," Alyssa assured her. "It's all over now. He won't try to find you or anything, because he knows we'll have him arrested. You didn't do anything wrong. You got out of there. And next time, you'll be a little smarter."

"There isn't going to be a next time, Alyssa," Katie said quietly. "I'm going home, where I can be safe. I think you should, too. This school is just feeding us a bunch of false hopes and lies. I think you should consider what you're dad's been telling you."

Alyssa snickered. "Safe? Is that what you think going home to Keith is going to make you? Well, let me tell you something, Katie. There's no such thing as safe. You say I should do what my dad says and find a job where there are no chances for disappointment? Well, I say that job doesn't exist. Anyone can lose their job. Anyone can be passed over for a promotion.

"And what do you know about what my dad is

telling me, anyway? Look, he may not agree with my being an actress in the musical theater, but he's never stopped me. He put me on the plane to New York to come here, didn't he? He just wants me to be happy. He doesn't want me to face a whole lot of rejection. No parent does. But my dad never said a word about my taking a job that was safe. How could he? He's in the army! He puts his life on the line all the time! The rest of us just have to pray he'll be okay."

Katie stared at Alyssa with surprise. She'd never heard her lose her cool and go off like that before. It was obvious that talking about her dad was a sore point with her. Suddenly Katie felt horrible about butting into an area of Alyssa's life. She was obviously not willing to open up about that.

"I'm sorry," Katie told her. "I didn't mean to . . ."

Alyssa softened. "I know you didn't. But do you see what I'm trying to say? You can't hide from pain, or disappointment. All you can do is get through it, and learn from it." She took a deep breath and tried to collect her thoughts. "Look, at least stay through the showcase, okay? Serena and I need you around. You made a commitment to us, and you've got keep to your word. I thought all Texans were men of honor."

Katie giggled despite herself. "Where'd ya hear that—in an old Western or something?"

"Sure, on the late, late movie. Some guy in a ten-gallon hat and a pair of boots said it. And you know I believe everything I see in the movies," Alyssa teased. Then she grew serious. "Katie, if you're not going to stay for yourself, stay for us. We can't do this piece without you."

Katie nodded in agreement. "You're hard to argue with, y'know," she said, trying to muster a small smile.

"So I've been told," Alyssa replied as she slowly began to unpack the rolled-up piles of hastily packed clothes in Katie's suitcase. She held up a short, purple and lime green sweater. "Besides, you weren't going anywhere with this," she reminded her. "It's the sweater you borrowed from me last week!"

Katie took one look at the sweater and began to giggle uncontrollably. She'd thrown the sweater in by mistake, with all of her own laundry. "You're right. I definitely have to stay. My wardrobe back home is much too boring. All those ten-gallon hats in my closet and all. Without your clothes to borrow, I'd be nothing."

Alyssa laughed and handed the sweater back to Katie. "Then I guess you owe me," she said.

"More than you'll ever know," Katie assured her.

Self-Expression Journal: Monday

I don't think I've ever felt more stupid than I did today. Here I thought I was so grown up, living on my own, making my own decisions, and I walked right into one of the oldest traps in the book. I guess I definitely got knocked down a few pegs—which is not necessarily a bad thing. I'll have a little more horse sense next time.

When Keith called tonight to see how the modeling shoot went, I told him I'd changed my mind and didn't do the shoot. He was so happy to think that he'd convinced me not to go through with it, and I just let him assume that that was how it had happened. I didn't exactly lie to him, but I didn't tell him the whole truth, either. There just didn't seem to be any point in upsetting him.

This is the first time I've ever kept anything from Keith. It feels strange and uncomfortable, like something between us is changing and I can't do anything to stop it. I want to be totally honest with Keith, I really do. But if I'd told him what had really happened in Lucas's studio today, he'd be on the next plane up here to drag me home—or worse, he'd tell my daddy what happened, and then they'd both be on the next plane up here. And I don't want to go home. I want to be in No Secrets. I want to be a star.

I know now that nobody is going to hand stardom to me. If there's one thing I learned today, it's that nothing really worthwhile is simply given to you. I'm gonna have to work for what I want. So first thing tomorrow morning I'm getting up early to put in some extra rehearsal time and work on my harmonies for the jazz piece Alyssa, Serena, and I are doing. I want to make sure I'm pulling my weight in this trio. Because if the three of us do our best in that showcase, we're gonna blow Miss Eileen Kerr away!

XXOO

Katie

Chapter 10

The phone rang beside Cass's bed. She glanced wearily at her alarm clock before lifting the receiver.

"Rise and shine, sleepyhead. It's time for your run!" The cheerful voice on the other end announced.

"Mom, you've got to be kidding!" Cass moaned. "It's not even six o'clock yet."

"The early bird catches the worm," Alana told her daughter. "Or in this case, the best trainer. I've arranged for Jake Bertrum to meet you at the school in twenty minutes for an early morning stretch and run. I noticed at our last rehearsal that your movements were a little stiff. I thought working out with Jake would make you more flexible. And you'll need the endurance you get from running if you're going to hold that high note for as long as we've planned."

Cass sighed. Her mother was right. If she was going to hold the high notes in "Greatest Love of All," she was going to have to get her lungs moving. Leave it to Kenny and her mother to find the hardest song

Whitney Houston had ever recorded, and dump it right into Cass's lap.

"Jake Bertrum has worked with all of the biggest names in showbiz. We're so very lucky that he's agreed to help us with this little problem. Come on, darling, wake up," Alana urged, this time with a slightly sterner voice. "We only have a few days until the showcase. And we're nowhere near where we should be."

Cass sat up and rubbed the sleep from her eyes.

"If I hang up now can I depend on you to be downstairs in twenty minutes?" Alana asked her daughter.

"Yes, Mom," Cass assured her. "I wouldn't let you down."

Cass was late getting to her choral seminar that morning. The workout with Jake Bertrum had left her muscles sore, and she'd lingered far longer in the shower than she should have. As she quietly slipped into the choral room she looked around for any unfamiliar face—the girls at PCBS had quickly figured out that anyone they didn't know could be one of Eileen Kerr's coaching scouts. Cass sighed with relief as she saw only the faces of her classmates standing behind their music stands. She knew Eileen Kerr's staff would frown on someone who was late, and she couldn't afford to lose points in their eyes.

Cass flashed Hannah a small smile as she took her place behind her in the second soprano section of the chorus. Hannah didn't return the grin. Instead, she stared intently on her music, refusing to make eye contact with Cass. But even without looking her in the eye Hannah, managed to notice how gaunt and pale Cass looked without her makeup on. It was obvious that Alana was working her daughter pretty hard these days, and the effort was taking its toll on Cass.

"Okay girls, let's try "Autumn in New York" one more time," ordered Ms. Lowe, the director of the choral seminar. She gave a nod to the class pianist, who immediately began playing the song.

When the girls had finished their rendition, Ms. Lowe pushed her glasses up on the bridge of her nose and frowned disdainfully. "That number is nowhere near ready for the showcase, girls. Altos, you weren't hitting your low notes the way you should. And the sopranos were off by at least half a beat. Worst of all, I felt no excitement from any of you."

"Maybe that's because your arrangement isn't exactly inspiring," Melanie suggested loudly.

"Excuse me?" Ms. Lowe asked angrily. "Did you say something, Ms. Sun?"

A quiet murmur went through the class as the girls spotted one of Eileen Kerr's people—a tall, lanky woman with a long black braid down her back—entering the classroom. Melanie saw the woman, too, but she didn't tone down her criticism on her behalf.

"I said, the arrangement is uninspiring. Y'know, dull. This is a new millennium. We should be trying new things. Maybe adding a few odd downbeats to some of the measures, or putting a little dissonance into some of the harmonies. Nothing major, but just enough to make the song stand out."

"I don't think 'Autumn In New York' needs your help in making it stand out. It's been a classic number in our fall showcases for years," Ms. Lowe said, dismissing Melanie's thoughts. The tone in her voice made it quite clear that it was time for Melanie to be quiet.

But Melanie wasn't giving in. "I think you need to get out of this building more often, Ms. Lowe," Melanie continued. "There's a new sound in the streets. Instead of being afraid of it, you should learn to embrace it. I'm not saying dump all the classics. I'm just saying it wouldn't hurt to blow the dust off of them and make them a little more interesting."

Before Ms. Lowe could respond to Melanie's tirade, the bell rang. The girls quickly swept up their sheet music and headed off to lunch.

Melanie walked out of the classroom alone. She had no desire to discuss her feelings with anyone just then. Her facial expression and determined, angry walk made it clear to everyone around that she wanted to be left to her own thoughts.

Unfortunately, Serena obviously didn't know how to read body language—or she refused to. She strutted right up to Melanie and matched her step for step. "Are you nuts?" she asked her finally. "Didn't you see one of those Omega representatives in the back of the room?"

Melanie shrugged. "So what?"

Serena stared at her in disbelief. "So what?! How do you think that little critique of yours went over with her? Don't you think she's going to tell Eileen Kerr what you did?"

Melanie snickered. "I repeat: So what?"

"You mean you don't care if you make No Secrets?" Serena asked her.

"I'm just not going to change who I am to do it," Melanie told her. "Besides, I'm not going to make No Secrets."

"How do you know that?"

Before Melanie could respond, Lexi came sauntering over toward the girls. "Well, haven't you two become buddies since our little evening's adventure," Lexi laughed in a haughty tone.

Melanie rolled her eyes. "We haven't seen a lot of you around here. Stopped by to change your clothes?"

Lexi smiled. "I guess I have been a little busy lately. But securing my place in No Secrets takes a lot of my time."

"Oh. What number are you doing for the showcase?" Serena asked with genuine interest.

"I'm not," Lexi told her. "I'm in the choral numbers and the general dance numbers. That's all that's required, isn't it?"

Serena nodded. "To pass for the semester, sure. But I thought you said you were working on getting into No Secrets. How're you going to do that without showing off your stuff onstage?"

Melanie rolled her eyes. Sometimes Serena's naïveté was absolutely frightening. "I think Lexi's been busy showing off her stuff somewhere else—right Lexi?"

Lexi didn't argue. "Well, Chet and I have been kinda busy working together," she admitted with a wink. "He's very aware of what kind of moves I can make."

"Oh my!" Serena blushed. "You mean you and that coach have been having sex?"

"Well, not exactly," Lexi admitted. "Not that I haven't tried. But Chet says that that's not professional. Still, we have been getting extremely close these days. And I don't think he's going to be able to resist my talents much longer."

Melanie glanced down at Lexi's white leather miniskirt and cobalt blue, low-cut belly shirt. It was an unusual outfit for the fall weather—but it fit Lexi's needs perfectly. After all, unlike the temperature outside, Lexi never seemed to cool down. "I'm sure he won't," Melanie agreed. "But it's funny, I haven't noticed Chet around here at all. I've seen all the other coaches, though."

"I know. Chet's sort of a back office kind of guy," Lexi explained. "I think he does a lot of the bookings and stuff. He'll be working at the brownstone, though, after Eileen has chosen the other seven girls."

Serena stared at Lexi with amazement. She didn't know which was more fascinating, Lexi's confidence or her method for getting chosen to be one of the eight finalists.

"Well, I'm off for another date with Chet," Lexi told the girls. "Catch ya later."

As Lexi sashayed down the hall, tears of indignation began to form in Serena's eyes. "It's just not fair!" she shouted out into the now empty hallway. "I've worked so hard, and I probably will never make No Secrets—just because that guy Chet saw me drunk. And it wasn't even my fault. But Lexi does absolutely nothing and—"

Melanie gave a haughty chuckle. "Oh, I wouldn't say she does absolutely nothing. She's suffered for her art. It's awfully chilly out to be wandering around in thong underwear and a miniskirt."

"I don't believe you! How can you think this is funny?" Serena demanded. "It's just plain unfair."

"Serena, look, if you want to join the pity party, the line forms over there. I don't want to hear it," Melanie said with a distinct lack of empathy. "Up until now, everything in your sweet little Midwestern fairy tale of a life has gone without a hitch. Well, welcome to the real world. You may be talented and smart, but sometimes that's not gonna get you where you want to go. Life sucks, and then you die. You may as well get used to it. I know I have."

Serena could feel the anger boiling up inside of her again. But this time she wasn't upset about Lexi. She was angry at whoever it was who had convinced Melanie that she didn't have a chance to make No Secrets. Melanie was so sure she didn't have a shot that she was determined to destroy any real chance she did have by doing things like fighting over musical arrangements with Ms. Lowe. It was a horrible self-fulfilling prophecy. Serena could only hope that Mel would shake that chip off of her shoulder before it weighed her down completely.

As Melanie quickly stormed away from Serena, Susie popped out from behind the studio door. She'd been straightening out her music folder and happened to have overheard the whole conversation between Mel and Serena. And boy was she was angry! Susie hopped out into the hallway and blocked Melanie's path. "Why'd you have to bark at her like that? Serena was just worried about you," Susie demanded as she raced up beside Melanie.

"I don't need anybody worrying about me," Melanie responded. "I've taken care of myself up until now, and I've done just fine."

"Yes, you have," Susie acknowledged. "But why should you have to deal with everything on your own? We're all your friends here. And we're all going through stuff."

"Yeah?" Melanie asked with accusation in her tone. "What have you had to go through?"

Susan grinned. "Are you kidding? I've had to work with Daria the past few days. Now if you ask me, that's what hell must be like."

Melanie laughed in spite of herself. That was just like Susie—using her rather unusual sense of humor to defuse any situation. "That is pretty bad," Melanie admitted. Then she sighed. "I guess I was a little hard on Serena. It's just that she's so wide-eyed and innocent all the time. Sometimes I just want to smack some sense into her."

Susie nodded. "I think that was what she was trying to do to you, Mel. She just wanted you to give yourself a fair chance with Eileen Kerr."

"That's something I never had," Melanie whispered sadly under her breath.

Self-Expression Journal Entry

I know we're supposed to be recording our own feelings in this book, but I feel like I have to write about everybody else's emotions right now. This place is getting too intense! Everybody's so stressed out about this No Secrets thing. We're all starting to crack. I almost walked into a genuine catfight this afternoon. I honestly thought Melanie was going to punch out Serena, right there in the hallway (which is something Mel could do with one hand tied behind her back, for sure). I mean I'll admit I was dumb to let Daria convince me to be part of her performance act, but at least I didn't mix it up with the toughest girl in the school. Now that's what I call really stupid! What was Serena thinking? I'm just glad I could calm Melanie down before things got any worse.

Okay, so now I'll write about my feelings (which is what I was supposed to be doing in the first place, right Ms. Lawrence?). I am totally burned out these days. Not from rehearsing or anything. I'm wiped because it's taken all my effort to hold back from letting Daria have it. She's making Janine and me insane. After Melanie's explosion in Choral Seminar today, Daria's become convinced that Melanie has lost any chance she might've had for making it into No Secrets. In Daria's sick little mind there's now one less girl to compete with for a spot at that No Secrets brownstone. She's more determined than ever that she's going to be one of the eight girls sleeping at that new address after Thanksgiving.

I think she's also determined to keep Janine and me from going to the brownstone with her. Every time we try to come up with an idea that might show off our talents a little bit, she finds a way to defeat it. I wouldn't be so angry except that she's tearing Janine's fragile ego to shreds in the process. Every time Janine tries to show her a better dance move or suggests a new harmony, Daria makes some crack about Janine's weight—like telling her that it might be better if she didn't turn her back to audience or something. Then Janine just crumbles and does whatever Daria says.

But I have a plan that will make Janine and I shine every bit as brightly as Daria during that showcase. It's going to take a lot of work on Janine and my part—not to mention a whole lot of sneaking around. But I think I can convince Janine that it'll be worth it.

Oh, and by the way, I've changed the spelling of my name. From now on, I'm calling myself Sioux-you know, like the Native American tribe? Kinda cool, huh? I've even made sure it looks that way in the showcase program. My mom's gonna have a fit, but I think it makes me sound exotic. It'll definitely catch Eileen Kerr's attention, which is, of course, totally my point.

More later.

Love,

Sioux ☺

Chapter 11

"Girls! You have got to be quiet backstage. If you can't contain your excitement now, how are you going to behave during a live performance when there's an audience sitting in those seats? This is going to be a disaster if you girls don't begin to act like the professionals you claim to want to be!"

Hannah rolled her eyes. This was her third year at PCBS, and it was also the third time she'd heard Madame Charlotte make that same speech. Every year the dress rehearsal for the showcase was complete and utter chaos. And still, every year, the actual performance went off without a hitch. Madame Charlotte knew that, the other teachers knew that, and the students knew that. Hannah had to wonder why Madame Charlotte wasted her breath year in and year out.

Melanie caught Hannah's expression and laughed. She knew exactly what her performance partner was thinking. And she agreed. "Let me guess. Next she's going to tell us about how the school's fine reputation is at stake, and how we have no right to destroy a

legacy by our giddiness and unprofessional behavior."
Melanie took on Madame Charlotte's faint French
accent as she spoke.

Madame Charlotte did not disappoint. As if right
on cue, she continued with her tirade. "Professional
Children's Boarding School has had a worldwide
reputation for more than forty years. I cannot believe
you are willing to put that reputation at risk with your
current giddy, unprofessional behavior."

Melanie and Hannah could not contain
themselves. The girls burst into hysterical laughter at
this latest outburst from their dance teacher.

"Ms. Sun! Ms. Linden! Do you two find something
funny? Perhaps you'd like to share it with the rest of
us. We'd all enjoy a good laugh."

"No, ma'am," Hannah assured her as she
desperately tried to stop laughing. Melanie bit the
inside of her cheek in an attempt to keep her giggles
from surfacing.

"All right, then. Let's work on the lighting for the
individual and small group performances. Alyssa
Wilkinson, Katie Marr, and Serena Barkin, please
come to the stage at once."

As Alyssa, Serena and Katie ran through their jazz
number, Janine and Sioux stood in a darkened corner
of the green room, whispering among themselves
while they waited for their turn. Daria stood across the
room, eyeing them with suspicious curiosity. Finally,
when she could stand it no longer, she moved like a
lioness stalking her prey, nearly pouncing on the two

other girls in her group. "What're you two so busy whispering about?" Daria demanded, her voice practically throwing darts.

"Nothing, Daria," Sioux told her. "Just the kinds of things friends talk about."

Daria didn't reply. She knew that Sioux was alluding to the fact that Daria really didn't have any actual confidantes at PCBS. But if the comment bothered Daria, she wasn't letting on.

"Well, as long as you're able to focus on our number when it's time to go on. I wasn't sure your backup harmonies were in key the last time we went over the 'She Works Hard for the Money' portion of the medley."

"Oh, they'll be fine, Daria. Don't worry. We won't let you down," Janine assured her. She lowered her eyes just slightly to avoid Daria's stare. "This dress rehearsal will go just as you planned."

As Daria walked away in triumph, Sioux whispered quietly in Janine's ear, "Of course the real performance may have a few surprises, though."

"Oh, just a few," Janine agreed.

"We're next," Melanie whispered to Hannah. "We'd better get to the backstage area."

"I thought we were scheduled to go on after Cass," Hannah said. "She hasn't rehearsed her number yet."

"Didn't you hear?" Melanie asked her. "Cass has been excused from the dress rehearsal—and from her classes for most of this week. Mommy dearest got her a doctor's note saying that any rehearsals other than the ones with her private vocal coach might strain her vocal chords."

"You've got to be kidding!" Hannah exclaimed.

Melanie shook her head. "Could I possibly make this one up?"

"Boy, talk about special privileges," Hannah muttered.

Melanie frowned. "What's the matter, princess? Are you bummed that someone other than you is getting special treatment for a change?"

Hannah usually tried to ignore Melanie's put-downs. She was almost afraid that if she began to yell or argue with Melanie, she would reveal something about herself that was better left hidden. But Hannah had had enough of Melanie's resentment. She put her hands on her hips and stared indignantly into Melanie's heavily made-up eyes. "I don't get any special treatment around here!" she insisted.

"But it's not because you haven't tried, princess."

"And don't call me princess!"

Before Melanie could answer, one of the stagehands raced into the green room. "Melanie and Hannah, you'd better get backstage. You're on in two!"

With that the feud ended as quickly as it had begun. Hannah and Melanie headed to the stage and began their performance. To the teachers and students who were watching, it appeared as though the two girls were the very best of friends.

But some of their classmates knew better.

"Maybe they should try acting instead of singing

for their showcase piece," Alyssa murmured from her seat in the back of the auditorium. "They're giving an Oscar-worthy performance up there right now!"

Self-Expression Journal Entry for the Third Week in November

Everyone sounded so excited about the dress rehearsal today. I feel really left out. I wasn't even there. I was off by myself in a studio on Seventy-second and Broadway, working out the final arrangements for my song with Kenny. It wasn't fun; it was pure work. But as my mother always says, 'Without hard work, you'll never get where you want to go.'

The trouble is, I'm not sure where it is I want to go. I think I want to be part of No Secrets, but I'm not as certain of that as the other girls around here are. They all think it'll be so glamorous and exciting to be part of a band. They've never experienced the schedule of a professional job. All the traveling, and hotels, and planes, and buses. It all sounds romantic to them. But I know the truth. It's just plain hard work. You always have to be on your best behavior, and no matter where you go you have to look absolutely perfect. Otherwise, you're letting the audience down. They have a right to have their illusions of glamour kept intact. After all, they're paying your salary.

Still, being in a group like No Secrets is what I've been working toward all my life. So I'm gonna give it my best shot and see what happens. Besides, being in an Omega Talent pop group might get my mom off my back for a while—I doubt Eileen Kerr would let her tour with the band.

Not that I don't love my mom. I really, really do. It's just that sometimes I'd like to be like every other seventeen-year-old on the planet—going places with friends, hanging out, and just vegging.

But with Mom it's work, work, work. And every day she takes me to these restaurants—the kind where I can be recognized by kids my age who remember me from The Kids Company. I think she gets a kick out of seeing me sign autographs for them. But all I keep thinking about is how much food I keep eating. If this keeps up, I'm going to be huge. And I can't let that happen. Huge doesn't go over real big in Hollywood—or in New York for that matter.

Oh no. There goes my cell phone. I'll bet it's mom again. I'd better pick it up before she discovers I'm slacking off.

Till later,

Cass

Chapter 12

"Errr! I hate this hair!" Alyssa's voice carried through the seventh-floor hall.

Janine poked her head out of her room. "'Lyss, is that you complaining about your hair again?" she called out.

Alyssa came padding out into the hallway in her bathrobe and yellow Tweety Bird slippers. "Just look at this, Janine," she moaned. "It's so boring! I need a new cut or something."

Janine laughed. "You've been saying that since the semester started and you haven't done a thing about it. You're in New York City. There are like a zillion hair salons here. Pick one, walk in, and get it done."

"I don't want to go just anywhere," Alyssa moaned.

Daria stepped out into the hallway and eyed Alyssa's hair. "Pardon me for eavesdropping," she apologized sarcastically. "Of course, it isn't really eavesdropping when you're screaming in the halls. But I think I can help. I've got a terrific little place in the East Village where I get my hair done. It usually takes weeks to get an appointment, but I'll bet I can get Andre to take you tomorrow—so you'll have a new do for the showcase."

Alyssa looked at Daria's stylish brown curls, and then felt her stick-straight dark hair. "I don't know, Daria. I mean we have very different hair, and—"

"Alyssa, give me a break. This is New York. Don't you think Andre has cut all kinds of hair by now? Trust me, he's wonderful. And he has this highlighting technique in which he uses a vegetable dye. Don't worry about a thing. I'll make the call for you."

Before Alyssa could answer, Daria was in her room calling for an appointment.

"Why is she being so nice?" Alyssa asked Janine. "She's up to something. You can count on it. And I'm afraid to take a chance, with Eileen Kerr coming to the showcase and all."

"Look, you need a haircut, right?" Janine reminded her. "And Daria's hair does always look fabulous—much as I hate to admit it. So her hairdresser must have talent. How bad can it be?"

"Well, I could lose my hair," Alyssa suggested.

"I hear bald is in this fall," Janine teased back.

Alyssa had to laugh. "I don't know. I still think I'm going to live to regret this."

At seven o'clock on Friday evening, Alyssa and Janine walked into Andre's salon on Waverly Place. The place was wild. Matchbox 20's latest single blared from the stereo system. And everywhere you looked there were trendy-dressed stylists clipping away.

"Can I help you?" a girl with short blond hair asked from behind the counter.

"I have a seven o'clock appointment with Andre," Alyssa replied.

"Okay, just go in the back and get changed, and he should be right with you."

Alyssa looked confused. "Get changed?" she asked.

The girl smiled. "There are robes back there. You might want to take off that pretty top. It says here you're getting an eggplant dye today, and we wouldn't want to stain anything."

As Janine and Alyssa walked toward the back of the shop, Alyssa asked, "What's an eggplant dye?"

Janine shrugged. "Didn't Daria say that they used vegetable dyes here for highlighting? Maybe that's just one of the vegetables they use."

Once Alyssa had put on the black robe over her jeans, everything began to happen quickly. A young assistant brought her to a chair to wait for Andre. The stylist arrived a few minutes later. Alyssa was surprised: He had close-cropped brown hair with long fringy bangs in the front. He certainly wasn't the type of stylist she imagined the classically coiffed Daria would go to.

"Daria says you're in the mood for a change," Andre told Alyssa.

"I guess so," she agreed somewhat reluctantly.

Andre smiled. "All right, then. Let's go in the back and give you those eggplant highlights."

Alyssa almost laughed. It was funny how excited hairdressers could get when you told them you wanted a change. It was like a challenge they could never refuse. "Sounds good to me," she told Andre.

"Oh, we're going to have such fun today!" the stylist assured her.

Janine went for a snack while Alyssa lay back with her head in a sink as Andre carefully placed a cap on her head and pulled various strands of hair through tiny holes in the cap. Then she waited while he went in the back and mixed up his vegetable concoction.

"Here we go!" Andre announced as he began to paint Alyssa's hair with a thick dye. "You must be the adventurous type," he added.

Alyssa frowned. "Who, me? Not really," she said. "I'm actually the most organized and steady one of my friends. Why?"

"Oh, nothing," Andre replied. "It's just that most girls who ask for eggplant highlights are a little more wild."

"Well, I'm not. I just felt like I needed a little change is all."

Andre worked silently for a while, concentrating fully on Alyssa's hair. Finally, he stood up and ripped off his plastic gloves with a great flourish. He reached over and grabbed a copy of that month's *Teen People*. "I'm all finished. The dye has to set for a while. Why don't you read, and then I'll be back in about half an hour to rinse it all out?"

Janine came back to the salon just as Andre was finished rinsing the dye from Alyssa's hair. She watched as her friend sat up and Andre began combing out the tangles. As she got a look at Alyssa in the bright salon lights, Janine's jaw dropped. "Uh, 'Lyss, remember when you said you wondered what Daria was up to?" she began.

"Yeah. I guess I was wrong. I mean, this place is amazing. So cool and hip. Maybe Daria is turning out to be okay after all."

Janine shook her head. "Don't jump to any radical conclusions."

"What do you mean?"

Janine gulped. "You haven't looked in a mirror yet, have you?"

Alyssa shook her head. "Nope. I've just been sitting here reading."

"Then you don't know."

"Know what?"

"Your hair . . . it's got purple highlights!"

Alyssa leaped out of her seat and raced over to a nearby mirror. Sure enough, strands of deep purple were scattered through her hair. "Aaagghhh! This is horrible!" she shouted at Andre. "What have you done to me?"

"Exactly what you asked," Andre replied. "I gave you eggplant highlights."

It was all coming together in Alyssa's mind now.

Eggplants were purple. The words "eggplant dye" had referred to the color of the dye, not what it was actually made of. This had been Daria's idea of a joke. "You'll have to change it back," Alyssa ordered Andre.

Andre shook his head. "No can do. That dye is very strong. If I try to add a second color to it now, it'll crack off, or worse . . ."

Alyssa could feel the blood rising to her cheeks as she realized that Daria had just sealed her fate for her. Purple-haired girls were not the kinds of singers a woman like Eileen Kerr was looking for. Omega Talent groups were not made up of East Village refugees. She'd never get into No Secrets now. To make matters worse, the showcase was tomorrow, and she couldn't go onstage like this.

"Well, that's it, I'm out of the showcase," Alyssa moaned to Janine.

"Now let's not freak out," Janine assured her, even as she herself was panicking for her friend. "There must be something we can do. Maybe get a wig."

"Where am I going to get a wig at this time of night?" she demanded. "And we have to be backstage in costume tomorrow by nine A.M.! I'll just have to go back and tell Katie and Serena that they'll have to work out something without me. It wouldn't be that hard. Their voices blend nicely. And with a few extra dance moves they could work on tonight—"

"Just cut it out!" Janine shouted at Alyssa with such force that she even scared herself. "You're not quitting the showcase. You're going on tomorrow, just as you'd planned."

"With this hair? Are you nuts? What'll Eileen Kerr think of this?"

"You know what, 'Lyss? I'm sick of hearing that woman's name," Janine declared suddenly.

"Are you kidding?" Alyssa demanded. "You know that tomorrow is the last chance we'll have to make a good impression on her. That's what makes it so important."

"No, it's not," Janine argued. "What makes it so important is that we've all worked hard and we deserve to be on that stage. We've all been so consumed with making the cut for No Secrets that we've forgotten the whole point of this performance is to entertain the audience. This isn't an audition, it's a show. And like you always tell everyone else, the show must go on."

Alyssa sighed. There was no arguing with logic like that.

Self-Expression Journal

I HATE DARIA Griffith.

Okay, that's about as close as I'm gonna get to losing my cool about this hair thing. Screaming and yelling and pitching a fit is just not my style. If my dad taught me one thing, it was to never let the enemy see you sweat. And from now on, Daria is my enemy.

I put on the greatest act this evening when I walked back into the dorms. I went right into Daria's room, smiled brightly, and thanked her. That's right, I thanked her. I lied and told her that this was exactly the change I was looking for. Something dramatic and different and totally wild. That really threw her off guard. She was sure I was going to be furious—which, of course, I was .on the inside. Oh, I'm gonna be one hell of an actress someday!

Katie and Serena have been great about the whole thing. Serena is even going to give me the purple boa she was supposed to wear with her costume, so that I can make a real statement. She actually thought my hair looked great. But I have a feeling Eileen Kerr isn't going to agree.

Janine sure put me in my place at the salon. I didn't know she had that kind of power in her. She's usually so soft-spoken and meek. It must've taken a lot of courage for her to actually yell at me. No matter what happens tomorrow, I'll always be grateful that she cared enough about me to let me have it.

Wish me luck tomorrow. I'm gonna need it.

Alyssa

P.S. Y'know, this self-expression journal thing isn't such a dumb idea after all. I actually feel better about things now!

Chapter 13

"I wish we didn't have to be first on the program," Janine moaned as she fastened the snap of her silky disco skirt behind her. "Why did they have to change things around? It's too much pressure."

"They put us at the top of the show because they knew we would start things off with a bang!" Daria assured her. "The teachers obviously have a lot of faith in my . . . I mean our talents. So just do everything the way we rehearsed it and we'll be fine."

"Oh Janine and I will do everything just the way we rehearsed it," Sioux assured her. She gave Janine a mischievous wink.

But Daria was too caught up in her own world to notice Sioux's gesture. "Good," Daria agreed in an authoritative voice. "I don't want anything to ruin this number. It's far too important . . . to all of us, of course," she added quickly.

As Daria walked away to check her makeup in a better light, Janine sidled up beside Sioux. "I don't know about this," she whispered. "I mean, what if

Daria's so thrown by the changes we made that she messes everything up?"

"Then she'll mess up," Sioux assured her. "And we'll look great."

Janine looked shocked at Sioux's sudden deviousness.

"Hey look, isn't that what she's been trying to do to us all along? We can play the same game she's been playing, Janine. Besides, Daria won't mess up. Despite being a jerk, she's got talent. And she's professional enough to just keep going no matter what happens. Just trust me on this."

"Sioux, Janine, and Daria, places now," the stage manager called. Quickly, the disco queens checked the laces on their jazz shoes, straightened their hair one last time, and ran out onstage.

"And . . . curtain," the stage manager whispered into her headset.

The curtain rose, and Janine, Sioux, and Daria got their first look at the audience. The lights were bright, and they could barely see past the first row, but the girls could sense that the people were there. They could feel their anticipation. The excitement ran through the girls like a shock wave.

"One, two, three, four," Daria counted down as the orchestra began to play.

"I will survive . . . ," Janine and Sioux sang out as they began their seventies disco medley. Then Daria picked up the lead vocal and moved around the stage as an old-fashioned disco ball scattered fractured light over her head. Daria felt confident and excited. Everything was going just as she'd planned.

But just as Daria headed toward stage left, Janine and Sioux broke into a heavily choreographed seventies hustle dance. Sioux twirled Janine around in a triple spin. Janine lifted Sioux in the air and did a pirouette on her toes. Sioux slid between Janine's legs and landed deftly on her knees. With each intense dance move, the audience's applause grew wilder.

At first Daria thought all of the applause was for her. She bowed in gratitude as she sang. But then, from the corner of her eye, she caught Janine and Sioux doing matching back handsprings and leaping up to dance some more. The look in her eyes was full of venom, but Daria managed to keep smiling.

When the song was over, Janine and Sioux ran offstage hand in hand. Daria followed close behind. "What the hell was that?" she hissed. "Why would you purposely try to screw up my song?"

"Because, Daria, it wasn't your song," Sioux informed her. "It was our song. And we just wanted to make sure the audience knew that! Besides, we were a hit. Didn't you hear that applause? It was amazing. Better than anything."

Daria couldn't argue with that. But she wasn't in any mood to agree with Janine, either. She simply stomped offstage and got ready to change into her dress for the all-school finale.

When Melanie sang the last note of "Open the

Lines," she bowed and drank in the thunderous applause. From the corner of her eye, Mel could see that Hannah was beaming. Melanie had to agree that Hannah had every right to be proud. There were some tough high notes in the song, and Hannah had managed to hit every one of them. Maybe Cass had actually done them all a favor by dropping out of the number. The song worked much better sung as a duet than it ever had as a trio.

And Cass had done all right for herself, too. Mel had to admit that her rendition of "Greatest Love of All" was possibly her best performance ever—and that was saying a lot considering how much experience Cass had. Melanie didn't want to admit it, but for once, Alana Morgan had done a good thing for all involved.

Still, as Melanie walked off the stage, she wasn't completely happy. She'd invited Julia to come to the showcase—she'd even put a ticket aside for her at the box office. But Julia hadn't come. Melanie didn't have to check at the box office to see if the ticket had been taken to figure that out. She just knew. Melanie and Julia had long ago worked out a signal so that Julia could let her know she was in the audience, supporting Melanie's playing. After each number, Julia would let out an ear-numbing wolf whistle. But today, all Melanie heard were cheers and the loud clapping of hands.

There was only one word that could describe the

scene in the dressing rooms after the PCBS Fall Showcase: bedlam. Clothes were flying everywhere as the girls quickly changed into their street clothes and got ready to meet the parents and friends who had come to New York just to see the performance.

Alyssa found her mom and dad in the school lobby right away. Her parents were hard to miss— especially her dad, who stood six foot three and was the only one wearing a dress military uniform.

Marcus Wilkinson hugged his daughter tightly. "You were amazing!" he complimented her. "You sang the blues just like Billie Holiday! Now why don't you go upstairs and wash that purple stuff from your hair? We're taking you out to celebrate!"

Alyssa kicked at the floor. "Well Dad, the thing is, this won't exactly wash out . . ." she stammered nervously.

"What?" her father demanded. "You dyed your hair purple?" He turned to his wife. "I knew something would go wrong if we let her come to New York by herself."

Lydia Wilkinson put a calming arm on her husband's shoulder. "Oh honey, it's not so bad. In fact, I kind of like it. Besides, it's not like Alyssa has gotten a tattoo or pierced her tongue or anything . . ." She paused in mid-thought and turned nervously toward her daughter. "You haven't, have you, Alyssa?"

Alyssa stuck her tongue out at her dad. "See, no piercings. And no tattoos, either. This was kind of a mistake, Dad. But it's only hair. It'll grow out."

"Well then, I guess there's nothing for me to do except take my purple-haired daughter out to a restaurant. Just do me a favor, willya honey?"

"Sure, Dad."

"Pick a place with dim lighting. Unless of course that hair glows in the dark."

Chapter 14

Melanie was in the seventh-floor bathroom putting on her makeup when she bumped into Katie. It was only about 6:30, but Katie was already in her sweatpants and carrying her text copy of *Hamlet*.

"Don't tell me you're going to study tonight?" Melanie asked her. "We just finished the best showcase in the history of this school. It's time to go out and PARTY!"

"I'm not in the mood," Katie said. "Besides, everybody's out with their folks."

"Yours didn't come?"

Katie shook her head. "But I already knew that they weren't coming. I just sorta hoped that Keith was gonna . . ." Her voice trailed off.

Melanie scanned the expression on Katie's face. It was easy to tell what had happened. "Didn't show, huh?"

Katie shook her head.

"Well hey, then he just gave you permission to come out with me and my cousin Charlie. He's pretty

118

cute. And while the cat's away—"

"No thanks, Mel. I'm just gonna stay here and study. Y'all go ahead and have a good time. Besides, I thought you'd be going out with Hannah tonight, to celebrate that great performance."

Melanie laughed. "Oh yeah, right. Me and the heiress. No way. In fact, I didn't even see her after the show. She swept off with her folks before anyone could even see them. I guess she wanted to keep them away from the riffraff around here."

"I am sort of curious about what her folks are really like," Katie admitted. "Do you think they're like the high society folks in those old nineteen forties black-and-white musicals?"

"Who knows?" Melanie replied. "And who cares? All I want to think about tonight is having a good time. You've got to come, Katie. I have to get a date for Charlie, or else he's gonna kill me. And if you don't help me out, I'll have to ask Daria. She's the only other one here who doesn't have anyone to hang with tonight."

"No, she's not," Katie whispered. "Look who else is still here." She pointed toward the hallway. Melanie poked her head out of the bathroom doorway just in time to see Lexi scurrying into her room with her head down.

"Where's she been all afternoon?" Melanie asked.

"I don't know," Katie replied. "She disappeared right after the showcase. I saw her walking away with Ms. Geoffries. Ask her if she wants to go with you. Charlie'd have a good time with her."

"Well, Lexi is more my cousin Charlie's type than Daria is," Melanie agreed.

"I don't think Daria is anyone's type," Katie added.

Melanie laughed. "Well listen, don't study too hard. Why don't you give Keith a call and find out what happened? He may've tried to get here and there was a delay at the airport or something."

Katie shook her head. "I doubt it. But it's worth a call. Now you get out of here and catch Lexi before she finds some new boy toy to play with."

Melanie headed down the hall. She wandered right into Lexi's room without knocking. "Hey Lexi, are you in the mood for—"

"Go away!" Lexi snapped without even turning around.

"What's the matter with you?" Melanie barked back.

Lexi turned around slowly. Her eyes were filled with tears. Long lines of wet, navy blue mascara covered her cheeks. In one swift motion she picked up a tabloid newspaper and threw it at Melanie. "That's what's the matter with me!"

Melanie looked at the paper. Right there on the front page was a huge picture of Lexi and Chet. Inserted into the photo was a snapshot of Eileen Kerr. The headline read, "Teenage Girls Will Do Anything to Be Eileen's Next Star."

"Oh man, *The National Reporter*. Talk about a sleazoid rag! I can't believe they hired a photographer to follow you and Chet around. I'll bet he was pretty mad. Did Eileen fire him?"

Lexi shook her head. "That would be impossible."

"Why?"

"Because Chet doesn't work for Eileen Kerr. Look at the reporter's name," Lexi said as she pointed to the small byline type at the top of the story.

Melanie glanced down at the paper. The reporter's name was Chet Barth. Oh man! Talk about making a bad call.

Chet hadn't been a coach at all.

"When we saw Chet with Eileen Kerr, it was because he was trying to get her to give him an interview," Lexi explained. "And when she wouldn't talk, he left and went to that Mexican restaurant."

"Yeah, but you'd think he would've told you he wasn't one of Eileen's coaches," Melanie insisted.

"You'd think," Lexi agreed. "But he didn't."

Melanie sighed. She knew why Chet had kept his mouth shut. He'd found a new angle for his article. Lexi had thrown a great story right into his lap . . . literally! No wonder he hadn't actually slept with her. It was probably against *The National Reporter* rules for one of their reporters to sleep with the underage focuses of a story. Gee, nice to know *The National Reporter* has a moral code, Mel thought sarcastically.

"Oh man. Has Ms. Geoffries seen this yet?" Melanie asked Lexi.

"Oh yeah. She's seen it all right. She's the one who showed it to me."

Melanie looked at the pile of clothes Lexi had

already dumped into a suitcase on the bed. She didn't have to ask how Ms. Geoffries had reacted.

"Geoffries said I'd broken so many school rules that she would've expelled me even if I hadn't dishonored the school in a national newspaper. So now I'm not only never going to be one of the No Secrets members, I'm out of PCBS. Back to Atlanta. Oh, I could just die. I can't wait to meet the 'rents at the airport. When Geoffries called them to tell them I'd been expelled, they were so angry! I don't think they'll ever let me out of the house again."

Melanie didn't know what to say. Part of her just wanted to give Lexi a hug or something to make her feel better. But the truth was Melanie wasn't a demonstrative person, and things like comfort hugs just didn't come naturally to her. So instead, she did what she did best: change the subject. "Well, how about we go out for one last total blowout before you go?" she asked cheerily. "You can do whatever you want tonight. No worries about curfews or school rules."

Lexi nodded sadly in agreement. "Sounds like a plan," she agreed. "I mean, what's the worst old lady Geoffries could do—expel me?"

Self-Expression Journal

I feel so bad about what happened to Lexi today. I mean, I don't agree with what she was trying to do——trying to sleep her way to the top was totally sleazy——but I think the punishment was pretty harsh. An article like that practically guaranteed Eileen Kerr was never going to let her be part of No Secrets—wouldn't that have been enough of a price to pay for what she did?

I'd be lying if I didn't admit that I was glad to find out that Chet wasn't one of Eileen Kerr's coaches. That means Eileen probably doesn't even know that Melanie and I were at that bar with Lexi when she met Chet. Nobody in Eileen's entourage saw me get drunk. So maybe I still have a shot at making the group (or at least at being one of the eight girls picked in the first cut, anyway).

I know I'm being kind of self-centered. I really should be focusing on feeling bad about Lexi. But I can't help it. Of course, I would never say anything like this out loud—it would just sound so horrible. I'm lucky I have this journal, so that there's one place I can let out my innermost thoughts, no matter how selfish they are.

Serena

Chapter 15

Alyssa and Janine sat together in the auditorium and held each other's hands tightly for moral support. Everyone was on edge. Usually when the whole school got together for an assembly, the room was buzzing with the sound of gossiping girls. But today, everyone was too nervous to talk. By the time this assembly ended, the lives of eight girls would change dramatically.

"What's taking her so long?" Daria snarled under her breath. "I thought a businesswoman like Eileen Kerr would be punctual."

"Maybe it's a tough decision to make," the girl next to her suggested. "There are one hundred fifty girls in the school to choose from."

Daria smiled. There may've been one hundred fifty girls in the school, but there were only about ten or eleven of them who had enough talent to impress someone as picky as Eileen Kerr. And with Lexi out of the running now, Daria's chances of being one of the eight semifinalists were pretty good.

After what seemed to be an eternity, Ms. Geoffries

walked out onto the stage and spoke into the microphone. "Before we begin, let me congratulate all of you on a brilliant Fall Showcase. I can't tell you all how proud of you I am. This was perhaps the best showcase the school has ever seen. Give yourselves a hand."

The girls went wild applauding their own efforts, and punctuating their clapping with loud whoops and cries.

"Just get to it already," Daria muttered under her breath.

As the cheers quieted down, Ms. Geoffries smiled. "But I know you all are anxious to hear from Eileen Kerr," she acknowledged. "And I don't think you should have to wait a moment longer. So, Eileen is here to announce the names of the eight girls who will go into serious training at the Omega brownstone. Four of these girls will eventually make it into the No Secrets band."

Eileen Kerr walked slowly onto the stage and smiled brightly at the girls in the audience. "First of all, let me tell you all how difficult of a decision this was. I came here to PCBS because I knew the school offered me a huge pool of talent from all over the country. But I had no idea just how incredibly professional and creative you all were. Choosing just eight of you to train with my staff and myself was one of the most difficult business decisions I have ever had to make.

"'Business' is the key word there. That's what this is all about. There are a lot of criteria I wanted to fulfill when choosing the eight girls. I was looking for a real mix of personalities and appearances, as well as singing and dancing styles. If you're not chosen, please don't take it personally. It's not a reflection of your talent or of your prospects for future success. It's just that you weren't quite what I needed for this group at this time."

The girls were growing more and more nervous with each of Eileen's words. The tension in the air was thick, and Eileen Kerr knew these girls couldn't take much more pressure. She opened her notebook.

"Will the following girls please report to Ms. Geoffries's office directly after this assembly, so that we can get the proper paperwork moving:

Cassidy Sanders,
Serena Barkin,
Melanie Sun,
Katie Marr,
Janine Gutierrez,
Hannah Linden,
Alyssa Wilkinson, and
Sioux Gregg."

That was it. Eileen left the stage, and suddenly all the tension in the room was broken. There were a few sniffles, and several disappointed sighs. But the screams of excitement from the eight girls who had been chosen to move to the brownstone over-shadowed everything else.

Lots of the other girls went over to congratulate the chosen eight. But Daria wasn't one of the gracious ones. She was furious with Janine and Sioux. As she passed by them on her way to class, she stopped and shot them an evil eye. Without a word, she kept moving.

"I'm sure glad we won't be coming back here after Thanksgiving," Janine said. "She'd be after my behind big time."

"Well, we won't have to see her—at least not for a while," Sioux agreed. "Remember, we're not in the group yet."

"No, not yet," Alyssa agreed as she turned around to give Sioux and Janine hugs. "But we're one step closer."

Chapter 16

"All right, I'm all packed up," Alyssa said as she flopped down on Janine's bed. "It's great that they'll move our stuff into the brownstone over the break. That's one less thing to do."

"I can hardly believe it," Janine said. "I never thought I would make it this far."

"Neither did I," Alyssa agreed. "'Specially with this hair. I thought I would die when Eileen told me that one of the reasons she picked me was that she was looking for someone who was daring enough to dye her hair to match her boa. Can you believe she wants me to keep it this way?"

Janine grinned. "I guess Daria did you a favor after all, though I doubt she sees it that way." She placed a pink sweater in her duffel and zipped the bag shut. "Okay, that's it for me. I'm ready to go out and celebrate. I think Melanie, Katie, and Serena are downstairs already. What about Cass and Sioux—are they coming?"

"Cass is going out to celebrate with her mother, I

think. And Sioux had to run down to Ms. Geoffries's office. I think she must've had some paperwork to finish up. She should be here in a few minutes. Let's go downstairs. She'll know to meet us in the lobby."

After waiting for Sioux for about twenty minutes, Hannah had just about had enough. "I can't stand waiting," she complained. "It's just bad breeding."

Melanie rolled her eyes. Despite the fact that she and Hannah worked well together onstage, there was definitely no love lost between the two of them. "I guess a dog like you has heard a lot about breeding," Melanie snapped.

Serena leaped in to keep the peace. "Look guys, we're going to be together a lot from now on. This fighting has to stop. How about we go upstairs and leave Sioux a note about where to meet us. "

"Don't bother."

Serena turned around to find Sioux walking down the stairs into the lobby. "Hey Sus, almost ready?" she asked.

"I'm not going," Sioux replied. "I don't exactly have a whole lot to celebrate at the moment."

"What're you talking about?" Janine asked her. "You were just handpicked by Eileen Kerr to try out for her new band. I think that's worth celebrating."

"It would be—if my parents hadn't just pulled me out of the running."

Janine's eyes grew large. "What're you talking about?"

"Weren't you listening? I said my parents didn't give

me permission to try out. Seems my dad just got transferred to Paris. The whole family leaves next week."

"Can't you stay at the brownstone while they're in Europe?" Alyssa suggested. "My dad travels all the time, and my family goes with him while I stay here. Come to think of it, this is the most stable home I've had in a while."

"I suggested that I could stay in New York," Sioux assured her. "But my 'rents don't want me to be an entire ocean away. They say it's too far. So, now I'm off to Paris."

"That doesn't sound too bad," Melanie offered gently. "Paris is supposed to be an amazing city."

"Lots of shopping, which is perfect for you," Serena teased, trying desperately to get her friend to see the bright side of things.

"I guess," Sioux agreed reluctantly. "And Eileen has offered to hook me up with a modeling agency over there."

Modeling! Katie shot Alyssa a nervous glance. Alyssa got her message loud and clear.

"As long as Eileen gave you the name of the agency, you know it's legit," Alyssa said quickly. "Just stick with the agency, okay? You know what they say about French photographers. An agency will protect you from getting into any trouble."

Alyssa looked over at Katie and flashed her a quiet, reassuring grin. Katie answered with a short nod. Hopefully they'd saved Sioux from running into any Frenchman that was even remotely like Lucas Harriman.

"Hey, maybe you'll even become the next Cameron Diaz. She got her start modeling in Paris. And the next thing anyone knew, she was dancing with Jim Carrey in *The Mask*," Janine suggested.

Melanie shot out her leg in an imitation of a karate move. "And beating up the bad guys with Charlie's other angels," she added.

"Well, Eileen did say she didn't think I'd have any trouble getting work in France, and she's a pretty good judge," Sioux admitted. "She says they love Americans over there—especially Americans with a few freckles."

"Well, then I'd believe her. Eileen has a pretty good track record with success," Alyssa said, trying to sound positive.

"Y'all are gonna be just fine," Katie assured her.

Sioux tried to muster a small smile. "Thanks, you guys. I'll send you a postcard and let you know how things are going. Right now, I've gotta go finish packing. My folks are coming in the morning to pick me up."

"Bon voyage," Alyssa said, trying to sound as cheerful as possible.

"If you become famous before we do, don't forget to help the little people who knew you when," Melanie teased.

"I could never forget you guys," Sioux assured her. "You're the best friends I've ever had." She turned away and dashed into the elevator before the tears started up again.

Sioux wasn't the only one crying. All of the girls

were misty eyed when those elevator doors closed. "I'm really going to miss her," Serena confessed. "But hey, at least I've still got you guys. It's going to be a lot of fun being alone in that big brownstone."

"That's true," Melanie agreed. "Now the only question is, who is Eileen Kerr going to choose to take Sioux's place?"

"Daria, I just want you to know that I have serious reservations about this decision," Eileen Kerr said in her typical straightforward manner. "It's not your talent that I'm concerned about. You have a wonderful voice, and I think your dancing can be easily brought up to a professional level."

Daria bristled at Eileen's brutal honesty, but said nothing. She didn't want to blow any chance she might have with the head of Omega Talent.

"Your main problem is an inability to be part of a team. That's crucial when you're a member of a pop group. Everyone must be able to trust you. My staff and I have seen you in action—and I'll tell you right now, there will be no back-stabbing in my brownstone. In fact, the only reason I am offering you the spot in the house that Sioux vacated was because I saw a glimmer of hope for your attitude during your showcase performance. The fact that you were able to share the stage on an equal basis with Janine and Sioux showed that perhaps you would be able to fit into No Secrets. I guess you could say that you owe your shot at the group to those two girls."

Daria smiled sweetly—as though the whole hustle choreography had been her idea in the first place. Eileen studied Daria's face suspiciously but didn't say anything.

"Should I go pack now?" Daria asked Eileen.

Eileen nodded. "Yes. I guess we'll see you at the brownstone on the Sunday after Thanksgiving. And Daria, even though you were the last girl chosen, I want to assure you that you have just as much of a chance of making the band as any of the other seven girls. All you have to do is work hard, and learn to play nice."

"You can count on me, Ms. Kerr," Daria assured her. "I'm really ready to be part of a team, now that I see how well it benefits everyone involved."

"Let's hope so," Eileen replied with just a twinge of doubt in her voice.

Chapter 17

"Well, at least we have each other," Serena told Janine as she took a bite of her turkey and stuffing.

"I never figured I'd be spending Thanksgiving in a diner in New York," Janine admitted.

"Me either," Serena agreed. "But, y'know, I thought I'd be kinda sad about being stuck at the school over the holiday, and I'm not. It's kind of exciting, actually. Different."

Janine nodded. "I know. I cried a little when my mom called this morning, but after that, I was fine. Besides, I think we'd better get used to things being really different. After all, there's nothing as unpredictable as being in a pop band. Of course, I know we're not in the band yet, but I can't help imagining what it would be like."

"Well, four of us are going to find out," Serena told Janine. "The question is, just who will be the final four?"

Self-Expression Journal

Well, here I go again, back to the grind of long rehearsals, never-ending image consultations, professional constructive criticism, and working with tutors instead of teachers. At least this time I'm with my friends. That is, if they're still my friends after the way I dumped them before the showcase. I'm really going to have to work hard to make that up to them. Just one more pressure to deal with, huh?

Oh well, I'm off to another Thanksgiving dinner. I think I'll stick to salad. I have to put on that leotard again first thing Monday!
Love,
Cass

Self-Expression Journal Entry

I can't believe I'm actually writing in this journal over the Thanksgiving vacation, but I'm really getting into this now.

My mom and dad and I had a big Thanksgiving dinner today—Mom always makes a huge fuss when Dad is around on Thanksgiving, ever since he missed that one during the Persian Gulf crisis. It's nice to have the whole family together. I was careful not to talk about No Secrets over dinner. I'm so excited about it, and I know my dad is trying to be enthusiastic, too, even *though he keeps telling me not to get my hopes up about being one of the final four.*

I know he's just trying to protect me, but I can't help but get my hopes up. This is the most important thing that has ever happened to me in my whole, entire life. I can't wait to move into that brownstone on Sunday night! I'll write more later,

Alyssa

Self-Expression Journal/Thanksgiving Weekend

Nothing ever changes around here. I told Mom and Dad that I was one of the eight finalists for No Secrets, and they were all business about it. Dad wanted to make sure that I ran the contract past one of his partners at the firm—someone named Dave, who specializes in entertainment law. And mom wanted to make sure that I didn't neglect my studies, just in case I changed my mind and decided I wanted to go to Harvard, her alma mater.

But college is definitely not on my mind right now. All I can think about is making sure I look better than the other girls in front of Eileen Kerr and her coaches. Oh sure, I'll be a team player—as long as the rest of them don't get in my way. I'm going to make this band, no matter what it takes!

Well, the next message you get from me will be from my room at the brownstone.

DARIA

Self-Expression Journal Entry

I think this had to be the worst Thanksgiving ever! The Aldens had about fifty people over for dinner, and I had to help Mom in the kitchen. By the time all the guests left, she and I had no strength to really eat anything. But Mom managed to save the wishbone for us to break together. I think she made sure I won. It doesn't take a psychic to figure out what I wished for, huh?

Well, I'm glad today is over. By Sunday night, I'll be working toward my new goal—making the band, and getting Mom out of this place.

Love,

Hannah

Self-Expression Journal Entry: Sunday

I was so excited when the plane touched down on good old Texas soil. It felt good to be home. Although now that I'm on the plane heading back to New York, I'm not so sure Texas is really home anymore. I mean, all Keith could talk about when he picked me up at the airport was my "New York-style" clothes, and how different I looked. That was really weird since when I'm in New York, everyone always talks about my accent and my boots, and how typically Texan I am. I'm not sure where I belong anymore.

But I can't focus on any of that right now. I have to focus on my work. Everyone knows Eileen Kerr expects her employees to give 150 percent at all times—and I've only got a few months to prove to her that I can do just that.

Wish me luck.

Katie

Self-Expression Journal

I just looked back at all my November entries. I can't believe how much has happened in the past few weeks!

I walked past the brownstone today. It's actually two brownstones that are attached by a stairway. It seems like any other building on West Eightieth Street, but looks can be deceiving. That building has magic inside. Eileen Kerr and her coaches are going to turn me into a star there. At least I hope they are. I can't believe how badly I want to be part of this band. I can't let anything get in my way.

Love,

Serena

——Yikes! I just read what I wrote. I'm beginning to sound like Daria. I'm going to have to watch myself. It's too easy to get caught up in the competition thing.

Self-Expression Journal Entry/
Thanksgiving Weekend

Most of the kids around here went off to a rave Friday night. Julia called and invited me, but something in her voice made it seem like she'd be just as happy if I didn't show up. So I didn't. Actually, there was a song in my head, and I wanted to write it down and work out the lyrics before I forgot it. So I was happy to stay home.

My mom and my aunt are both really excited about my being one of the eight girls Eileen picked, but my mom was careful to warn me about the temptations that come with being a success in the music business. That's pretty ironic, since she succumbed to a lot of those temptations without having had any success at all. Still, I know she's just trying to spare me some of the problems she faced when she was my age, and I have to give her credit for that. She's actually turning out to be an okay mom after all.

Well, that's it for now. Sorry this was so boring, but I'll bet my next journal entries will be really interesting!

Peace out!

Melanie

Self-Expression Journal

This is the last entry I'll ever write from my dorm room at PCBS. At least I hope it is—if I don't make the group, I'll probably have to wind up back here again. Of course, I don't want to think that way; I'm trying to follow Alyssa's advice and stay positive. Not that that's going to be easy with Daria around. I don't know who I feel worse for—Susie (oops, I mean Sioux), or the rest of us who are now stuck with Daria because of it. (I just hope Daria doesn't wind up being my roommate. I can just see her checking my jeans size and broadcasting it to everyone else in the brownstone.)

I'm going to a dance class tomorrow morning, first thing. I don't want to waste a whole weekend just lying around. I need to be in top condition when I get to the brownstone. Besides, I'm so nervous, I need a good workout to get rid of all this tension.

It just seems so weird that when everyone gets back here on Monday, I won't be here. I'll be at the brownstone—and there will only be eight of us there. But it's even weirder to think that in just a few months, it will only be four of us. And all I can think about is, will I be one of those four?

Longer
Letter
Later,

Janine

Katie shut the door and plopped down on her bed. Then she opened the bag and pulled out the long, white, rectangular box inside. Tears welled up in her eyes as she saw the bright red letters on the box: EARLY PREGNANCY DETECTION.

Katie had been in a state of denial for at least a week now. She kept hoping that the next day would be the day her period came. But that never happened. Now here it was December 31, and Katie just couldn't face the New Year without knowing.

find out what happens to Katie and the other 7 finalists in...

no secrets
The Story of a Girl Band

★2 Sneaking Around

by Nancy Krulik

for more information about this book,
visit our website at
www.penguinputnam.com